MW01612028

This novella is dedicated to–

*everyone fighting the losing battle to protect
the Earth for possible future generations*

*and Yoshimitsu Banno.
You tried to warn us... but nobody listened.*

GOTTERDAMMERUNG

by Constantine Furman
based on a general idea by Yoshimitsu Banno

GOTTERDAMMERUNG

ISBN-10: B0DYYRPRBL
ISBN-13: 979-8308702894

Though inspired by some real people and events [historical or otherwise], this is ultimately a work of [predicative] fiction. All the characters, character names, and events portrayed in this book have been changed or exaggerated drastically for dramatic effect and/or ghoulish overkill. Otherwise, they are either products of the author's imagination or are used fictitiously. All the events depicted are fictitious. Any similarity to events, persons, or situations, in actuality, living or dead are purely coincidental.

Special thanks to David Silliman for his invaluable help.

Please leave a rating and/or review at your Amazon.com (or other book website) of choice. It really helps.

TABLE OF CONTENTS

CHAPTER 1 - The Family Whisenhunt

By the year 2050, the Earth had become nothing short of a disaster zone. Factory smokestacks without number belched smoke into the air on a daily basis. Crowded rush-hour traffic on highways sent dangerous levels of carbon monoxide skyward.

An appalling amount of trash and waste began to float on top of the ocean. The Great Pacific Garbage Patch had become an actual floating island of garbage capable of landing upon. Oil slicks drifted on top of the oceans' waves across the globe.

Cities were experiencing the worst crisis of overcrowding in human history. The planet's resources were woefully overused and the fracking caused by drilling machines did immeasurable damage inside the crust.

For all intents and purposes, mankind had seemed to consciously try to destroy their planet.

In Los Angeles, California, a house with a chain-link fence surrounding it sat innocuously in a seemingly normal suburban-style neighborhood. However behind the home, a quartet of factories were visible in the distance and shot soot into the air. The result of intrusion of the sky's air was a low-level smog.

Inside the house, an 8-year-old girl with reddish brown hair and a white-haired, short older woman sat at a grand piano. The little girl played the massive instrument like a pro, her fingers tickling the ivories into a masterful rendition of *Fur Elise*. The elderly teacher slowly nodded her head with approval as she listened to the tune emanating from the piano before her.

Suddenly in the middle of the piece, the little girl stopped playing and began to have a coughing fit. The older woman looked up and noticed her front door was open. She rushed over as fast as her legs would move her and slammed the door shut.

"Oh, I'm so sorry about that, Gertie," the piano teacher gasped remorsefully. A few moments later, the little girl stopped her coughing. She looked up at her teacher and gave a tired shrug.

Amongst the hubbub of L.A. sat the APFE ("All Purpose For Everyone") Medical Center, a sprawling health clinic with plenty of parking that was currently sparsely filled. In the distance behind it was a large factory that had no less than three smokestacks floating dark grey smoke into the air.

Inside the center's laboratory, sundry medical men milled about. Laboratory paraphernalia littered the room. Clear and murky liquids alike bubbled like caldrons in glass tubes.

The chief physician here was Dr. Richard Whisenhunt [whiz-en-hunt], a gaunt 47-year-old man with neatly-styled balding blonde hair. He had a square-shaped face with a strong jaw line, medium-sized almond-shaped blue eyes, and resting bitch face. He wore a burnt umbra-colored suit beneath his paint-white lab coat. Around him working with the lab equipment were his assistants, Michael, Sam, and

Thom, all of whom were at least 10 years younger or maybe half his age.

"I can't believe some of the things these people think..." Whisenhunt spoke in a loud, blustery voice that commanded attention. "There is no doubt that this Reichlenn is an important find. It's certainly a remarkable additive. But they're already touting it as the solution for the world's food shortages!"

"The first few trials have been very positive, Dr. Whisenhunt," Michael said defensively. "They've shown a rate of two to three times normal growth when this chemical is used."

"Indeed, this Reichlenn data is impressive," Thom agreed.

"Michael's right," Sam chimed in. "What if this really is the solution to our current food situation?"

On one of the lab tables sat a notebook full of data on the Reichlenn Growth Hormone and its effect on the size of grain. It showed that the grain grew at least five times bigger than normal.

"The solution?!" Whisenhunt retorted as he began to walk about the lab. "I'm afraid this 'solution' would only create more problems for us. What do you think will happen if mankind consumes this chemical over a long period of time? We have no idea what strange effects it could have on us. Possibly cancer, or even worse! Everything causes cancer nowadays. This talk of it being a real solution to world hunger is just nonsense. They're just trading one looming crisis for another."

"But the trial period is nearly completed," Michael spoke up, "and the government wants our reports—"

"Then we'll just have to start over," the head doctor interrupted. "No, using Reichlenn to grow large food quantities would only cause even more problems that we'd have to deal with later on. You'll find it's not so easy as just spreading some fertilizer around. Remember DDT or Agent Orange? Nature has its own way of running things and mankind can't expect to just change them without facing dire consequences in the future."

Simultaneously, a jet zoomed in from the smog-ridden, dingy-looking sky for a landing at LAX Airport. After the jet had successfully landed and taxied its way into position to stop, its passengers were permitted to exit the plane and head for the terminal. Among them was one Jonathan Lerman, a 25-year-old young man carrying a pair of cases of luggage in each hand.

He had medium-length, tousled brown hair and a friendly smile on his rounded, boyish face. His eyes were light brown and his eyebrows were slightly unruly. His softly-rounded features made him look a bit younger than he actually was. His body was tall and lanky like it never quite filled out. His deep blue, short-sleeved t-shirt was wrinkled, giving away the fact he'd been flying for some time. The jeans he was wearing were not as noticeable.

As Jonathan exited the plane, he was taken aback by the quality of the air in the sky. He scanned

his eyes across it to study the discolor but then
continued moving ahead.

At a small dance studio in downtown L.A.,
young girls practiced dancing ballet-style as a slow,
romantic melody played over the sound system. Each
child moved in complete synchronicity as the others
and the movement themselves were as smooth as
water. Each were dressed uniformly in dark blue ballet
leotards.

Overseeing them all was 23-year-old Phoebe
Whisenhunt. Phoebe had shoulder-length, wavy dark
hair that framed her face perfectly. She had a smooth,
oval-shaped face with a broad forehead, a straight
nose that rounded at the end, and strikingly blue,
almond-shaped eyes. Her cheeks were softly rounded
and when coupled with her friendly smile gave her a
warm and approachable demeanor. Her body was
shapely and svelte with noticeably long dancer's legs.
She wore a white sleeveless spandex top that clung to
her body for dear life and showed off her toned arms
and a pair of loose-fitting blue jeans but was currently
barefoot.

"One, two, three, four..." the dance teacher
counted off in a soft, dainty voice. "One, two three,
four." The children all lifted their right leg in accord-
ance with Phoebe's cadence. "Just a bit longer, girls.
You're doing great... now, all of you reach into the air
and slowly drop your arms out to your sides," she lead
by example as she spoke and the children followed
suit. "Well done, everyone, now chill."

The children lowered their still-raised legs and relaxed. In a nearby mirror, Phoebe noticed Jonathan walk into a room. She reacted with an open-mouthed grin before turning around, running his way, then jumping onto him, clamping her arms and legs around his upper body. Jonathan backed up a step to keep his balance.

"Whoa, hold on there!" Jonathan reacted. "Mind my poor spine, will ya? Did you gain weight while I was gone??"

"I have not!" Phoebe scoffed as she play-hit his chest.

"I'd forgotten just how excitable you are."

"You've been away forever!" the dance teacher continued. "Did you miss me?"

"Every damn day," the young man replied. "Every damn night too, for that matter."

"Jon, there's kids here," Phoebe admonished.

"Oh, like they ain't heard worse," he volleyed back with a smile as he set his girlfriend back onto the ground. "How's your leg doing?"

"It's fine," Phoebe flatly said as she stiffened her left leg and shook it slightly. "The bone's healed up as well as expected. Doctor says I can't dance anymore, but what does he know, eh? That's not going to stop me from teaching others the awesome power of dance," she declared as she stiffly struck a 5th Position pose. Jonathan chuckled in response.

"I think Phoebe's his girl," one of the young girls whispered to the girl next to her, but obviously loud enough that the adults could hear.

"Excuse me, young lady," Jonathan spoke up, lifting up his left hand for attention, "but Phoebe belongs to no one. I, however, *do* belong to her." Phoebe involuntarily grin-chuckled. "She's gotta bill a' sale an' everything."

"Teacher and new guy sittin' in a tree..." two other girls chanted together through a wide grin they tried to hide by lowering their faces.

Jonathan leaned over Phoebe's way. "I think your kids think you're a slut, honey," he said in a low voice as the two girls finished off with "K-I-S-S-I-N-G." Phoebe's mouth dropped in shock as she looked over at him with an expression of offended incredulousness.

Meanwhile on a sidewalk near a busy city street, 45-year-old Europa Whisenhunt carried two paper bags of groceries as she made her way back home. She had shoulder-length, wavy dyed blonde hair that fell naturally around her face, an oval-shaped face with a smooth complexion, the result of makeup successfully hiding her aging. She had a high forehead and almond-shaped blue eyes whose color popped. Her nose was straight and her lips curved into a warm, genuine smile that made her seem gentle and friendly. Her left hand was adorned with stylish, eye-catching rings on each finger. Her straight-backed posture conveyed a sense of elegance and confidence. She wore a tight, puce-colored flowery top, a brown belt at her waist, and a black skirt that went down to her upper calves.

Europa came to a stop as she saw that she was passing next to an antique shop and decided to bounce in for a quick browse seeing as her food wouldn't spoil *that* quickly. She just started to move a step when—

"Hey mama," a voice spoke up behind her. "Wanna homeschool me some luuuuuuuuv?"

Europa's face switched to some mix of outrage and plain old rage as she turned to see where the voice came from. Standing on the sidewalk nearby was a plain-looking dirty blond-haired teenage boy, no older than 19, wearing a long black overcoat with a red band around his left arm. Europa realized this could go any number of bad ways, but proceeded to gulp that down as she bent over to set her groceries on the ground against the side of the antique shop's wall.

As she stood back up, Europa grinned warmly at the incel-nazi before her, even thrusting out her chest a little for extra distraction. The boy grinned as he realized this was easier than he thought. Europa slowly walked over to the boy's position with maximum seduction oozing from each hip-thrusted step.

"Easy, baby," the incel-nazi tried to coolly push back. "I mean, we can do it here if you like, but—"

When Europa made it within range, she suddenly sucker punched the kid straight between the eyes, knocking him flat on his back. Workers and patrons inside the nearby antique shop ran to the window to see the furor.

Before the boy could get his bearings again, Europa stepped onto the pair of jeans underneath his coat, landing the heel of her brown pumps directly where his genitals would be.

"You probably like this, don'tcha, punk?" Europa spat as she pushed her foot in deeper. The pained groaning and writhing of his prone body made it pretty obvious he did not. "You know what you do when you run into a Nazi bastard like you?" she rhetorically questioned. The only response was more pained grunting and some plaintive cries for help. "You punch them right in their smug, stupid face," Europa continued. "Every. Goddamn. Time." She bent down and swung with her left arm, managing to knock the incel-nazi out cold.

As Europa stood back to her feet, she kicked the boy in the side for good measure. Some of the people inside the antique store slowly shook their heads and clapped with admiration.

CHAPTER 2 - Earth 2050's State of Affairs

In the waiting lobby of he APFE Medical
Center, children of varying ages sat impatiently with
their mothers, each waiting to be seen in turn. The
younger children were all wearing COVID-style air
masks. One little girl coughed irritably. Thom
suddenly appeared on the scene and walked over to
the girl. He bent over and held out some candy-
looking lozenges for her.

"That's quite a cough you have there," the lab
assistant warmly observed. "Here, these lozenges may
help you feel better."

"Thank you, sir," the mother replied. Thom
gave her a quick smile as the little girl took the lozenge
in her mouth. He then set about distributing the same
candy-medicines to all the other absolutely miserable
children.

"What kind of bullshit is this?!" Whisenhunt's
voice blasted out from within his office, grabbing
everyone's attention. Some mothers gasped as they
heard the profanity. Others covered their children's
ears far too late. "Get outta here!" the doctor
demanded.

Inside Whisenhunt's office, he sat behind a
cluttered desk that looked like things were just placed
on top of each other haphazardly. The walls were a
deep bronze-colored wood paneling. They were judi-
ciously decorated with either images of unblemished
landscapes or landscapes being polluted or the factories themselves responsible for the pollution. He also
had a medical-looking poster up except it featured

animals that had gone extinct: dinosaurs, saber-toothed tigers, the dodo, Stellar's sea cow, the auk, the moa, the pyrenean ibex, the Tasmanian Tiger, and lastly an image of a human couple with a question mark beside it.

Standing across from the incensed physician were Officers Brandt and Richter, both impeccably dressed in their deep blue uniforms. "Now, just calm down a minute," Brandt tried to begin with an outstretched arm.

"Calm down?" Whisenhunt parroted. "Who's interrupting whom here? I think I'm being quite calm considering the circumstances."

"You've repeatedly done this over the past few months," Brandt stated.

"And you're worrying the owner," Richter added.

Brandt dug out some photographs from a manila envelope he had under his left arm then handed them over to Whisenhunt. As the doctor flipped through them, he saw they were pictures of a small Piper Archer airplane passing very low over a smoke-billowing factory.

"We have these photos here," Brandt continued to make his case. "They're proof of what you've been doing, Dr. Whisenhunt."

"So you're supposed to be policemen..." the doctor grumbled. "Is the factory paying you to harass me?"

"We're only doing our job, sir," Richter shot back.

"Yes, I chartered the Archer and flew a few close inspections on the plant," Whisenhunt explained. "You'd be better off investigating them, yes?" He pushed his chair back and rose to his feet, still carrying the photographs in his left hand. "The amount of pollution it's pumping into the air is still far too much," he continued. "It may appear to be lessened, but it's still doing damage to our atmosphere!"

"Not true, sir," Brandt contradicted. "The factory emissions are well within the limits laid down by the law."

"If that's a fact," Whisenhunt countered, "then what the hell's making all these people here sick?"

"You're just making ridiculous assumptions!" Richter scoffed dismissively.

"I'm a scientist," Whisenhunt declared. He really wanted to punctuate that statement with the word "motherfucker," but good sense got the better of him. "I deal in facts. Facts!" he belted out as he opened the door to his office. "Have a look at what's going on for yourself," he commanded as he pointed to the children waiting to see him. "There! What do you think all these people are ill from? It's not just Los Angeles, but this is happening all over the world in heavy industrial areas. Detroit, Guangzhou, Dehli... The children here can hardly breathe. They're having to go to school wearing masks to keep the filthy air out of their lungs! How about asking their parents what they think of these limits laid down by the law? Go on, just ask that poor mother over there what she thinks of the pollution making her little girl sick!" he challenged, pointing to one of the mothers outside before turning to hold out the pictures to the officers. "And take your damn photographs too. Here."

"Come on," Brandt exasperatedly sighed to Richter as he took the photos out of Whisenhunt's hand.

Just then, Jonathan and Phoebe made their way into the waiting lobby. She now wore a black leather jacket over the clothes she was wearing at the dance studio.

"What's all that commotion?" the young man inquired.

"Ehhh..." Phoebe groaned a reply. "Sounds like my dad tellin' the police ta get bent again."

No sooner than she said as such did Officers Brandt and Richter pass by them, making a beeline for the exit. Jonathan and Phoebe, meanwhile, strolled into Whisenhunt's office as the doctor ruminated at his desk, angrily pushing and pulling on a slinky like a grumpy kid.

"Daddy!" Phoebe called out as she entered the office.

Whisenhunt's mood immediately 180'd and his face switched to a warm grin as he spied his daughter. "Hey, I know that girl!" he joshed. "Gimme a hug!" Phoebe complied and smashed herself into her father for an embrace. After a moment, he looked up to see Jonathan standing nearby.

"Where's *my* hug," the boy questioned, causing Whisenhunt to crack up into a laugh.

"It's good to see you, Jon," the doctor said as his daughter let go of him. "But I don't hug dudes."

Jonathan silently giggled. "I don't know what the deal is with you guys huggin' each other now."

"It's called emotional security," Jonathan teased. "Look into it." He then sat on a nearby couch as Whisenhunt parked it on his desk.

"So how was Africa?" the doctor inquired. "Can't imagine it's that great."

"Things are really awful there," Jonathan explained. "But I've got some good photographs. *National Geographic* plans to run some next issue."

"Impressive," Whisenhunt said with legitimate respect in his voice. "Tell us all about over dinner later cause I've got an absolute ass-load of patients out there."

Jonathan looked up and noticed a photograph of a polluting factory on the office wall. "Oh," the young man began. "I'd been away so long... As soon as I got back, I noticed that the sky is a lot clearer here."

"Now don't you go believin' that too," Whisenhunt rebuked. "The pollution is even more dangerous here because we can't even see it in the air. Did you know that in America alone, we're losing twenty-six species of birds a year to the dirty air? The last Bald Eagle and California Condor went three months back."

"What?!" Jonathan spat back incredulously.

"I heard that the other day on the news," Phoebe interjected.

"Mmm," her father grunted. "A report I read said ten million people starved to death last year alone. If that's true, seven to nineteen people die every day.

Five to thirteen people every minute... and four to twelve people die of hunger every second."

"Jesus!" Phoebe exclaimed with genuine repulsion in her voice, clutching at her own chest.

"That's nothing, Phoebe," Whisenhunt continued. "There are rivers around the world that once provided enough fish and produce to feed communities for generations that are now almost lifeless with nothing in them fit for human consumption... because of runoff from blue jean factories alone."

Phoebe suddenly felt a wave of guilt come over her because she liked blue jeans. The office door swung open and Michael hurriedly entered. "Sorry to interrupt, sir," the assistant began. "But we just got a call. Some strange creatures have been discovered outside a' town."

"Creatures... ? What creatures?" Whisenhunt demanded to know.

"The caller said they look like giant earth-worms," Michael explained.

"Alright, let's go there now an' see what's happenin'," the doctor ordered. "Get the car ready."

"What about your patients?" Jonathan pointed out what should've been obvious.

"Get Thom on 'em!" Whisenhunt snapped his fingers at Michael.

"Right," the assistant answered as he charged back out of the office followed close behind by the doctor. Jonathan quickly got up to follow.

"And where do you think yer goin'?" Phoebe questioned with a shrug.

"I'm goin' with 'em," the young man retorted. "You should come too. This may turn out some good stuff."

"But why?" Phoebe whined. "You just got here and now you're running off again??"

"It's my job, Phoebes," Jonathan responded. "I'm a photographer!" He then rushed out of the room leaving his girlfriend behind.

"Oh, Jonathan, who'd ever want to see pictures of giant worms?" the young woman grumbled aloud to herself before apprehensively following the others.

Out in the parking lot, Dr. Whisenhunt, Michael, and Jonathan ran for Whisenhunt's vehicle, a shiny emerald green Chevrolet Equinox EV gas-free electric car. Phoebe trailed behind.

"Get us there!" Whisenhunt called out to Michael, tossing the car fob his way.

"We'll bypass the freeway," Michael said as he caught the fob. "I know a shortcut."

"Hurry it up, Phoebes!" Jonathan admonished. "Get them dancer legs movin'!"

"Wait a minute... !" Phoebe responded. "One of them doesn't work right."

The foursome piled into the Equinox, Michael and Whisenhunt up front and Jonathan and Phoebe in back. Michael started the engine with the car's fob, revved the engine, then zoomed away as fast as he could.

As Whisenhunt's car cranked down a city street, Jonathan surveyed the area they zipped past.

Having finally made its way to the rural grass-land in question, Whisenhunt's car came screeching to a halt. Nearby were all kinds of emergency vehicles—Red Cross trucks, military jeeps, ambulances, etc. The noise of an amassed crowd could be heard as the foursome exited the Equinox. A contained fire could be seen just ahead.

"Outta the way!" Jonathan said to no one in particularly in an effort to get through the crowd.

"C'mon, let us through here!" Whisenhunt bellowed as he and Jonathan pushed their way through the crowd. They came to a sudden halt as they were blocked by a trio of no-nonsense soldiers keeping the crowd back.

"Lemme through!" Whisenhunt shouted.

Other soldiers nearby were blasting flame-throwers across the area at something. Both police and news helicopters circled overhead. The people in the crowd on land desperately tried to see what was going on.

"Get back!" one soldier commanded as he pushed on the crowd. "Come on, get back!"

More blasts of flamethrowers shot through the immediate area. Whisenhunt advanced quickly, ignoring the fiery blitz around him, having managed to make his way past the soldiers alone.

"Come on, clear the area!" another soldier called out. "We need a clean shot!"

Jonathan and Phoebe followed after the scientist.

"Get those flamethrowers goin'!" another soldier directed.

As she advanced, Phoebe noticed something ahead of her and stopped short with a shriek. Giant earthworms slithered about ahead of her, some making their way out of the ground. They were a light orange almost beige color and looked like a cross between a ribbed snake and a sperm cell. Their head was blank and emotionless with no sign of eyes or a mouth. Their bodies were around ten feet in length.

Phoebe tried to pull her legs away, but one sneaky worm had managed to slink up to her position. The thing swiftly wrapped itself around her legs and lower waist, causing her to fall to the ground with a scream. Phoebe groaned as she tried to pull herself free. The worm's head menacingly closed in on her face and Phoebe froze with terror, not even able to verbalize her fright.

Just before whatever the worm wanted could happen, a soldier rushed in and kicked the worm off Phoebe, causing it to skid across the ground. Seconds later, another soldier kneeled onto the ground next to Phoebe and fired a flamethrower, roasting the accosting worm in moments. Phoebe sighed with relief as she watched the thing die.

Jonathan snapped off photo after photo, too distracted by the spectacle of it all to notice what was going on with Phoebe.

"Clear the area!" a soldier called out. "I said clear the area!"

Dr. Whisenhunt, meanwhile, had managed to close in on the unit's commander and was taking him to task.

"I'm sorry, sir," the commander said, "but I've been given orders to make sure these creatures are destroyed!"

"How is that gonna help us?!" the doctor challenged. "You gotta catch one first! We gotta find out what caused these monstrosities! Get it right, man!"

Whisenhunt tried to run after one of the worms in the distance, but the Commander grabbed and restrained him. A lick of flame shot out of a flamethrower nearby.

"Oh, no you don't!" the commander groaned. "Get back here!"

"Doctor, don't... !" Michael shouted on deaf ears.

"Stop it, we've got to get one!" Whisenhunt tried to explain. "We've got to study these things!"

"Hold him! Keep him here!" the commander shouted to an underling. "Don't let him go out there!"

It was probably for the best as a holocaust of flame washed over the giant earthworms leaving little more than writhing pulp behind.

"Smells like burnt play-doh..." Jonathan observed.

CHAPTER 3 - Food for Thought

That evening in the Whisenhunts' kitchen, the doctor, Jonathan, Phoebe, and Europa sat around a large table having a steak dinner. Phoebe had changed into a cute, purple blouse. All four had wine glasses filled to various levels.

"You alright, kid?" Whisenhunt queried, leaning over near his daughter's ear.

"Yeah, sure," Phoebe retorted. "Just gonna have nightmares the rest a' my life is all." Her father grimaced.

"What, did Africa tighten up your belly?" Europa admonished as she noticed how little Jonathan was eating. "You gotta make up for lost meals. Fill up your plate, boy!"

"Thanks," Jonathan said between bites. "I bet the Africans would be more than happy to have a barbequed earthworm or two. Better than nothing, don't you think?"

"That's gross!" Phoebe whined.

"They looked really juicy and full of protein. Right, Doc?" Jonathan pressed, ignoring his girl-friend's protests.

"That's even more gross!" Phoebe doubled down as Europa nodded her head.

"Phoebe's right; that is gross, so hush it," Whisenhunt stated in a deadpan manner. "But still, we can't be sure what those worms were made of or what made them grow so big. Here in America, how many of us can even tell what it is in the food that we eat anymore?"

"Thanks, Monsanto..." Europa grumbled in a low voice that only Whisenhunt seemed to hear as evident by his grin.

"But we still have to eat it..." Jonathan replied.

"Yeah, we really don't have much of a choice," the doctor agreed. "All of our food is poisoned to one degree or another. It's just a question of how much. The 'deregulation' republicans are always baying about just means 'I get to poison you as long as it's profitable'."

"Did you ever hear of something called AF-2?" Europa queried as she pushed a fry into her mouth.

"Yeah," Whisenhunt answered. "They called it a new miracle preservative when it hit the market," he explained as he took a drink of wine. "It was an anti-bacteria chemical and it worked well so they stuck it in a lot of food without taking time to think about it."

"They put it in a lot of fish, I thought?" Europa pressed.

"Yeah. Lotta fish," her husband replied. "'Specially in Japan. They used it to keep food from spoiling so quickly. But pretty soon into its usage, they found something seriously wrong with it."

"This AF-2 sounds like that chemical you've been studying," Phoebe observed.

"Almost exactly," her father confirmed. "AF-2 was a popular food preservative for a long time. Then, they found out that it caused incurable cellular damage to those who consumed it. People were poisoned for years by the very food they ate. That's why I can't let them just put Reichlenn on the market."

Jonathan took a good long look at the piece of meat on his fork. He looked over to find Europa doing the same. She looked at him and shrugged.

"By the time they banned it," Whisenhunt continued, "it had already been used for many years. I think that was... 1974 or somewhere around there. But it was cheap and it worked, so they used it. A lot of people think like that."

Europa gave up and decided to just call it a meal for the night, cleaning her mouth with a cloth napkin.

"With those kinds of people in charge," the doctor surmised, "things just get worse and worse until no one knows what to do."

"If human beings were gone from the Earth," Phoebe pondered aloud, "would the world, like... heal itself?"

Her father chuckled briefly. "That may be right..." he answered. "Back when COVID first hit and we all had to stay indoors, the Earth's environment started healing itself in a hurry. But nobody cared. You can already see the Earth striking back against us. Remember the typhoons in southeast Asia and when New Orleans was destroyed by hurricanes? Or that time when there was a tornado *inside* of a hurricane?? And all the recent earthquakes all over the world? I mean, really, earthquakes in Oklahoma? Since when is *that* a thing?"

The house phone began to ring in another room. Europa got up from the table to go answer. Her husband turned his neck around to watch her leave. "Hey..." he began in a low voice. "Now that your mom's occupied, tell me... you kids plan on getting married?"

Whisenhunt's sudden prying grabbed Phoebe and Jonathan's attention. Phoebe nearly choked on her wine. "You mean together?" she absent-mindedly asked.

Whisenhunt squinted his eyes, then turned to look over at Jonathan. "You got something you wanna tell us, boy?"

"I am so confused right now," Jonathan admitted with his hands held up.

Phoebe cleared her throat then recomposed herself. "Don't you think that's interfering, Dad?"

"Well, maybe," the doctor sighed. "Although, when two people are in love, I don't see why they shouldn't be able to settle down... Have kids... Vote responsibly."

"But with things as crazy as they are..." Jonathan stammered.

Whisenhunt chuckled again. "You're right to be worried," he admitted. "But Europa really wants a grandkid."

"You mean right now?!" Jonathan flippantly replied. "Kinda busy eatin' here."

Phoebe grimaced, then turned and smacked her boyfriend in the arm.

"Some people are working hard out there to ruin the world," Whisenhunt explained. "Somebody's gotta be the counterbalance to do good things."

Europa returned to the kitchen and sat down in her chair next to Phoebe. "Alright, everyone can relax. I'm back," she announced. "What'd I miss?"

"Who was that?" Whisenhunt inquired.

"Am I happy with my long-distance carrier?" his wife listlessly sighed.

"What'd you tell 'em?"

"Only when they're not botherin' me when I'm tryin' ta spend time with my family."

"Attagirl."

"Wait a minute," Jonathan interrupted. "What do you mean 'people are working hard to ruin the world'?"

"Nobody seems to care about taking care of this blue little planet of ours," Whisenhunt answered. "You've seen the state of things. It's not happening on its own. We're doing it. And the things we're doing can get scary."

"Example," Jonathan challenged.

"Well," Whisenhunt thought aloud as he rubbed his chin. "You hear some years back about that guy in Texas that died?"

"You're gonna hafta be more specific," both Phoebe and Jonathan said in unison. When they were done, they turned and looked at each other both surprised. Europa leaned forward to take a sip of wine.

"This guy in Texas, he just goes outside, right?" Whisenhunt began. "Dies. No heart attack, no stroke, nothin'. Just dies... Because of the *heat*."

Phoebe and Jonathan looked at one another again, this time with disbelief.

"The Earth is getting hotter and more unstable every year," the doctor explained.

"Just like Phoebe," Jonathan gently nodded.

"Hey!" Phoebe protested.

"We have screwed up the planet's climate so badly," Whisenhunt continued, "that air conditioners are no longer a luxury.... They are an absolute necessity to get through the summer! Every damn year. And not just in the usual suspects of Texas and Arizona, but everywhere in the world now. They discovered a drought warning stone some time back in the Czech Republic. It was dated as being carved in the 1600s. And on it, it had the message to us, here in the future: 'If you see me... weep'. And that's not to mention that cliff some industrialist blew up in the Middle East to renovate for some real estate deal or something. The cliff had what they thought were the numbers '1-3-5-$\sqrt{}$-5' carved into it in old-timey writing. Only, it didn't actually say one-three-five-divided by-five... It said 'J-E-S-U-S'—Jesus... We curse ourselves with our own hubris."

Phoebe, Jonathan, and Europa all sat motionless, shifty-eyeing one another. "Well, that's not ominous at all," Europa finally spoke up.

"Human beings are the only creatures on Earth who do not recognize their place on it," the doctor began again. "This planet was not made for us and does not exist solely for our sake. It is not for us to conquer and pillage, but rather to work together for the mutual benefit for all life. The plants and animals are said to glorify God by simply being what they are and fulfilling their natural roles; only we have decided that our role is to lord over creation, exploit and sacrifice it at the altar of our shortsighted ambitions.

It's way past the time to say enough. The Earth will only take so much. It only remains for us to decide: shall we embrace it or follow our egos to extinction?"

The other members of the Whisenhunt family just sat there looking at each other.

"I'm gonna need more wine," Europa finally broke the silence before rising to her feet.

Meanwhile, at the White House in Washington D.C., Madame President Erica Cady sat looking out the window behind the presidential desk staring off into nothing in particular. Cady was a white woman in her late thirties with thick wavy brown hair and wore a stylish deep blue woman's business suit.

With her were two Cabinet members Jergens and Chiang—both middle-aged men. Tsking once, President Cady turned and looked to her subordinates.

"Giant worms..." Cady began with a sigh. "Why did it hafta be giant worms? You know, I was really hoping I could end my term more quietly than this."

"That's what the reports say, Madame President," Jergens replied.

"Do we know what it was that caused them?" she pressed.

"We're not exactly sure," Jergens answered. "But our insiders say that it may have to do with some chemical spillage that happened in the area in the late 90s."

"The news will only cause panic," Chiang added. "Besides, the worms were all wiped out completely. Even if there are some left somewhere, we can't even be sure they actually pose any kind of threat."

"Yes, but if they do," Cady sighed with resignation. "Please, let's keep this hush-hush... at least for the meantime."

"We'll try our best, Madame President," Chiang said, "but apparently there was someone there trying to investigate it. Luckily, the commander there was able to keep him out of it."

"Who?" the president said more than asked.

"Local fella by the name of Richard Whisenhunt," Jergens responded. "He's a... well, I'm not really sure what he is." Erica tilted her head up as she listened. "He's like a... scientist-doctor or something. He's involved with scientific R&D in Los Angeles, but also he's got a practice. Not sure how that works or why he won't stay in his lane, but..."

President Cady huffed as she looked off into the distance. "Whisenhunt, huh? Where have I heard that name before... ?"

CHAPTER 4 - Long Day's Journey Into Night

The next morning, Phoebe and Jonathan sat around the dinner table eating breakfast—the old standby of bacon and eggs. They didn't speak and were predominately occupied with their meal. Europa milled about behind them attending to counter matters.

After a bit, Whisenhunt rounded a corner, ready for the day in a light blue dress shirt and brown slacks. He fastened up a black tie as he advanced.

"Morning, Dad!" Phoebe greeted with a mouthful of food.

"Mornin', sunshine," he shot back.

Europa appeared in front of Whisenhunt out of nowhere to greet her husband with a plate of breakfast—pancakes, bacon, and sausage—and a kiss.

"Morning, darling," the doctor mumbled as Europa pulled away. He took his plate and sat down next to Phoebe.

"Did you sleep well?" she inquired before ingesting a piece of bacon.

"Didn't get too much sleep, I'm afraid..." her father answered. "But we... got off eventually." He turned and winked at Europa, causing her to simper and turn away with embarrassment.

"Are you gonna go out and discover anything for the world today, Doctor?" Jonathan questioned like it was a big deal.

"Nah, not today," the doctor said as he forked in some sausage. "I'm off to Seattle for a meeting. Some of my colleagues are gonna smack down some science on them jabronis. You guys gonna be here when I get back?"

"Well, I live here, so I'll have to be," Europa said with maximum snark as she continued her rounds in the kitchen.

"I'm afraid we won't, Dad," Phoebe more reasonably replied. "Jonathan and I are going to visit his parents. We'll be gone for a few days."

"Yeah and we'd better get going, Phoebes," Jonathan groaned as he got to his feet.

"Okay," she acquiesced. Both Phoebe and Jonathan left the table with their dishes. Phoebe gave her mother a hug. "Bye, mom," she said. "Hold down the fort for us."

"Those dust bunnies are goin' down," Europa stated in a Charles Bronson-esque cadence as she let go of her daughter.

As Jonathan stood by, Phoebe headed over to her dad to give him a hug as he still ate breakfast. "Take care in Seattle," she said as she pulled herself into him.

"I will," her father replied. "You as well, sweetheart."

"And uh... try not to punch anybody again, 'kay?"

"I can't make that promise, sweetie."

"Whoa, wait a minute..." Jonathan spoke up. "I think I missed somethin' here. What's this about you punching somebody?" Whisenhunt cleared his throat like he wanted them to shut up about it.

"Dad was on Sean Hannity's show," Phoebe began. "And Hannity was pretty much making fun of him 'cause of global warming and them being in the middle of a snowstorm. You know, how they call it 'global warming' when it's really climate change?"

"Yeah?" her boyfriend said more than asked.

"Well," Phoebe continued. "Finally Dad asked—and it was *soooo* awesome—he asked, 'Sir, are you legally retarded'?"

Europa shook her head to herself as she returned from a closet with a broom, unable to keep herself both from chuckling or smiling.

"I stand by what I said," Whisenhunt announced as he cleaned his mouth with a cloth napkin.

"And Hannity kept being an insufferable dick," Phoebe recounted. "And finally Dad wound up hauling off and punching him in front of the whole damn country."

"I don't stand by that," Whisenhunt said as he stood up from the table.

"I do," Europa chimed in. "He was bein' an ass."

"Got 'im on John Oliver's show the next week," Phoebe added. "When Fox tried to sue, the judge threw the case out of court cause he was like 'We all saw what happened'. I believe the phrase 'I'd have done the same thing' is in the court records." She involuntarily chuckled as she finished the last sentence.

"Wow..." Jonathan flatly said. "Well, with that, we'd better be off, Phoebes." He turned and held his hand out toward Whisenhunt. After looking down at it and realizing what was happening, he shook it.

"Take care of my little girl while she's gone," he said.

"I'll guard her with my life, Doctor," the young man flippantly replied.

"You damn well better," Whisenhunt sternly countered. He then stared Jonathan down, Eastwood-style. Moments later, Whisenhunt cracked up laughing, joined in by Phoebe, and eventually Jonathan too. Europa smiled to herself as she swept up nearby.

Later that day at the environmental meeting in a hotel convention room in Seattle, the panel was headed by a trio of serious-looking scientists. The first was Dr. Plotkin, a skeletal botanist with dark hair. The second was Dr. Lynne, a wider zoologist with greying black hair and the tallest of the three. Lastly was Dr. Whisenhunt. Above them was a placard that read "*Mankind and the Environmental Future.*"

The convention room was filled nearly to the brim with concerned citizens of all types and ages. Dr. Plotkin spoke to the room with authority and carried a pointer, standing next to a series of slides showing weathered or otherwise polluted landscapes.

"As you can see," Plotkin pointed out, "We are destroying these ecosystems that provide us with beauty and clean air to breathe as if we *want* to make things harder on ourselves. It's not a matter of sentimentality to protect our environment. Without these complex ecosystems, we will not continue to survive. In the past, people held nature to be sacred, but not any more. They were thinking in the right direction way back then. Just you look... these places that had been protected are now being systematically destroyed... and we're all responsible for it! Our beautiful shores of sand and trees have continually been disappearing—down through the centuries until today. The consequences of economic growth has raised its ugly head. Americans have become careless of nature. Entire species of wildlife are being wiped out forever and for what? The pursuit of material wealth? This is what we get for thinking only of ourselves." He punctuated that last sentence by striking the panel table with his pointer to drive home the point. It caused the nearby Dr. Lynne to jolt back.

A middle-aged housewife stood up to take umbrage. "But what do you expect us to do?" she demanded to know. "We don't control the companies or businessmen that do these things. Do you expect us to hold ourselves responsible every time B.P. ruins a coastline?"

"Of course not," Whisenhunt replied, still sitting at the table. Plotkin took the time to sit back down next to his colleagues. "But what you're talking about is only one part of a larger problem. Over the past few decades, population has steadily decreased and is continuing to drop to dangerous levels. Women are refusing to reproduce—and who could blame them, honestly? But with reproduction diminishing so does the human race. But to say that each of them bears no responsibility for the health of the people in this country is absurd. We have to look beyond ourselves to do what needs to be done to keep the balance of nature and mankind in check."

A young man barely out of high school stood to his feet. "Doctor?" he called out for attention.

"Yes?" Whisenhunt turned his attention toward him.

"Even with cities like Seattle becoming too large," the young man began. "Our technology is constantly advancing. Don't you think that we could overcome these problems using new technologies?"

Whisenhunt pointed to Dr. Lynne to turn everyone's attention toward him. The zoologist rose up behind the table to take center stage.

"Change of this magnitude, I'm afraid, is not quite so simple," the scientist explained. "Whilst Dr. Whisenhunt is correct that birth rates are dropping, overpopulation is still being a problem across the globe, chiefly due to a lack of resources that cause its own set of problems."

Dr. Lynne raised his hand outward, which caused new slides to appear, these of mice in varying sociological developments.

"In this experiment," Lynne began, "a group of mice were given plenty of food and water. Their population increased rapidly. The mice are quick to react to their overpopulation and we can easily see its effect on them." The slides began to reflect visually what Dr. Lynne was explaining. "The males began to fight amongst themselves," he continued. "The females became neurotic and began grouping in the corners. New mothers would devour their own offspring. Soon, they find the answer to their overpopulation problems—and the cage is littered with their dead."

The people in the meeting watched and listened with ever-growing grim expressions and reactions. These findings did not sit well with them at all.

"This example applies well to human beings when their cities become overpopulated," Lynne still spoke. "The same symptoms are present there too. When a city is overpopulated, it should be considered unfit for habitation and abandoned by its citizenry."

"But we're human beings for God's sake!" a middle-aged man didn't even bother standing to speak. "We're not rats! It has taken us centuries to get to our level of civilization. It would take us years more to start again. What? You think we should just throw it all away and just forget it?!"

Whisenhunt stood up to take over as Lynne sat back down. "I don't think the solution is as drastic as that, but we certainly have to think about it," he replied. "Already our 'technological advances' have done immeasurable damage to our planet and more damage is being done all the time. The Earth is being poisoned by continual pollution with cadmium, mercury, and things of that sort. The threat to our survival is far too great. Even the oceans—they're choking on the filth that has been dumped into our seas!"

A smog-filled sky hovered over the shore of a seaside town in Northern California and the polluted ocean that stretched out before it. Non-degradable industrial waste rocked on the surface of the water and clashed with the deeper colors of the red tide that had appeared.

A crowd of local fishermen stood watching from the shore. At their feet lay scores of dead or dying fish that had beached themselves to get out of the poisoned water. The ones still flopping about were moments from death, though.

Among the crowd were Jonathan, his father Will, his mother Bernica, his teenage sister Abril, and Phoebe. Phoebe was visibly ill about what she was seeing. Their visit was, at best, going off the rails. One of the other women there wept uncontrollably.

"Stop crying, fool," one of the fishermen balked. "Tears can't help us now."

The onlookers there were all varying degrees of forlorn. Jonathan looked like someone just told him his puppy was dead. Tears streaked down Phoebe's face.

"We can't go out into the sea for food any more..." a woman observed.

"Of course we can..." a nearby fisherman chided. "We have to. The seas have given us our livelihood."

"The seas are polluted..." another voice began.

"The fish are dead..."

"And I'm still in debt with my boat."

Will Lerman, a larger, more stately-looking version of Jonathan, dressed in light blue jeans and a green work shirt, slowly began to advance toward the ocean. When he got to the water past the dead fish, he did not stop.

"Your dad, Jon..." Phoebe pointed out. The other fishermen began to murmur amongst themselves about what he was doing.

"What are you doing?" one questioned.

"Wait, come back here!" Bernice called out. "You don't know what's in there!"

Jonathan ran out after him, his quick movements causing water to splash every which way. Will just ignored his advance as he progressed into the sea.

"Dad, come back!" Jonathan yelled to his father. "Stop, Dad!"

As Jonathan tried to take hold on him, Will fought off his son.

"Are you nuts?!" the young man said more than asked. "Why are you going out there?!"

Finally, Will came to a stop. He turned to look at his son, a gravely serious look on his face. Bernice, Abril, and Phoebe seemed horrified as they watched from land.

"Why am I doing this?" Will answered with a question. "What else is there to do?! Can't you see without the sea and its animals, our lives are over?" Jonathan did not know what to make of this statement. Will, however, was not feeling generous enough to explain and turned to start out into the sea once again.

"It's no good, Dad!" Jonathan yelled. "Come back to land!"

"They took the fish..." Will declared. "Now they can take *me*!"

That night, Phoebe stood next to one of the many beached boats, staring out into the Pacific. She looked visibly upset by what transpired throughout the day.

Eventually, Jonathan ran out to the shoreline. As soon as he appeared, Phoebe snapped back to reality and looked his way. "How's your father?" she softly inquired.

Jonathan turned his head about several directions before finally finding Phoebe in the shadows nearby. He began to walk over her way.

"Better now," the young man answered. "We finally managed to get him off to sleep."

"Poor guy," Phoebe shook her head and clicked her tongue. "It's lovely, isn't it?" she finally said after about fifteen seconds that felt more like minutes to the two.

"What's that?" her boyfriend asked for clarification.

"It's still beautiful..." Phoebe pressed. "Hard to believe the sea is so polluted. It's filled with the screams of dying fish. I can hear them, Jon..." Jonathan reacted with visibly rude skepticism. "Maybe this is a message to humans..." his girlfriend continued. "To see what's happened to them won't also happen to us. When I was a child, I was so dumb. I never paid much attention to the things my dad told me about the Earth."

"I don't think 'dumb' is the right word," Jonathan pointed out. "Can't expect a kid to know how to save the world. That's too unreasonable. We read about these disasters or watch them on TV. They fail to see until it happens to them—like how my dad suffered today. There must be thousands like him. As I stopped my father from killing himself today, I thought to myself that maybe mankind itself is really starting to go insane. Things are certainly getting worse, but I don't think it's the end of the world. That's a bridge too far."

"I think mankind will survive this," Phoebe spoke up.

"Why's that?

"Well, if people are the cause of the problems, then they could also be the solution."

"Suppose man goes batshit crazy first and wipes itself out?"

"Stop that," Phoebe balked. "Where's your faith? Whenever I think mankind is headed over the edge, I just remember men like my father and then I see that they can change things. As long as we try, there will always be hope, Jon."

Jonathan turned to look out into the sea to consider what he'd just been told. Phoebe, meanwhile, lowered her head and stared at the sand at her feet. "It's a lonely old night..." she half-mumbled. "But aren't they all?"

"What're you talking about?" Jonathan said more than asked. "I'm right here."

"Are you?" Phoebe pressed.

Jonathan didn't understand what her game was. All he could manage was to stammer out a "Yeah..."

The two slowly advanced toward one another. Phoebe walked like her left leg was limping. Once within touching distance, Jonathan leaned down and kissed Phoebe.

"Mmm, you taste good," he observed. "Savory."

"That's your mom's dinner, dude," Phoebe shot back.

"Well, then..." Jonathan muttered. "Gimme some sugar, baby."

The couple closed in for a kiss once again and its passion increased monumentally. Phoebe could feel the endorphins drift into her brain, which seemed to push out her concerns about the dead fish in the ocean. But then, she suddenly realized she couldn't breathe.

"Jnn..." she garbled. Jonathan was not paying attention. Phoebe suddenly yanked her head back and with it an audible wet smack sound as their mouths detached. She then started to breathe heavily.

"What is it?" her boyfriend inquired.

"Jesus, Jon!" Phoebe gasped between breaths. "You don't have to eat my face! You forget how ta kiss while you were gone?"

Jonathan noticed how dangerously out of breath Phoebe legitimately was. "S-sorry," he stammered.

Phoebe looked up at her boyfriend, then turned her head around, seeing the beached boat above them. "Get me up in one a' these boats an' I'll show ya right," she stated with a coy grin.

"Never keep a gal waiting," Jonathan replied.

In the Lerman house up the hill from the shoreline, Jonathan's sister Abril stood looking out into the sea through the home's screen door. After a few moments, her mother ambled over next to her.

"I think Jon just knocked up the girlfriend," Abril matter-of-factly stated.

"What's wrong with you???" the matriarch hissed. "Go on; get outta here. Go ta bed."

Jonathan and Phoebe lie next to each other in the bow of one of the sturdier boats gazing up into the sky.

"I kinda wanna smoke..." Phoebe thought aloud.

"You know, I think your students were right," Jonathan finally blurted out. "Good girls don't know how ta do all *that*..."

Phoebe lightly smacked him across the chest with her bare arm, not even bothering to look his way. "Not funny," she admonished breathlessly.

CHAPTER 5 - Ch-Ch-Ch-Ch-Changes

Science continued on the march in Los Angeles' APFE Medical Center. Richard Whisenhunt eyeballed a liquid in a test tube. He shook it around then gave it another look like he expected it to do something. "I can wait as long as you can," he grumbled to it.

His assistant Sam Markham stood nearby, rather ashamed-looking.

"So the bank turned down your loan?" Whisenhunt said more than asked.

"Y-yes, Doctor," the assistant replied.

"Isn't that just lovely?" Whisenhunt began. "We bail out Wall Street, Citibank, and car factories after they cripple our nation... *twice*, and when it comes right down to it, they can't help people that actually need it."

"Yeah, they refused to help in any way," Sam explained. "So, that's why I've come to you."

"I don't know if I can be of any help..." the doctor surmised. "You're looking at most of the money I get from the government. And Europa surely doesn't own the fancy jewelry she deserves."

"But, I'm only asking for a little bit..." Sam pleaded. "Just some to save up and help my daughter, Sara."

"I get it," Whisenhunt sighed. "Well... I have no alternative... but to see to it you get a raise. Okay?"

"Doctor... !" Sam gasped.

The doctor went back to looking over his experiments. "Think nothing of it," he said. "I'm happy to do it. 'Specially for a soon-ta-be grandfather."

"Doctor, you don't know how much I appreciate this," the assistant informed.

"I don't think I've ever seen you this excited before," Whisenhunt replied.

"Eh, if I stumble onto a way to make Reichlenn non-lethal to human beings, just you wait and see," Sam said with more gusto in his voice.

"Hallelujah!" Whisenhunt cheered.

"I really can't believe people are just trying to push it out on the market," Sam continued.

"For having such education, it's amazing just how foolish scientists can be," the doctor said. "They make discoveries and find half-truths and move blindingly ahead in the name of progress before thinking about the ramifications of their actions. Just because we can doesn't mean we should, but a lot of my colleagues don't seem to think about that."

"Well..." Sam muttered. "At least you got them to decide against cloning dinosaurs. Can you imagine how bad *that* would have been?"

"Yes, I can," Whisenhunt fired back. "I've seen the movies. You'd think they did too."

Clouds over the African sky looked discolored. There were steely shades of grey, as well as dark blues, dank greens, and purple flourishes.

"Satellites report an alarming rise in radioactivity over Madagascar," a British newsman for the BBC informed. "An atomic-layered cloud cover blankets that area and is now moving east toward Asian population centers. Doctors report widespread hallucinations by the native populations. The U.N. is dispatching a team of scientists there to investigate."

Whisenhunt and Michael stood in a parking lot at LAX International with his other assistant Thom and Dr. Patrice Sherman, an attractive woman dressed in a white-trimmed red business suit. She wore glasses at the top of her button nose and had short but thick hair that framed her face perfectly.

"You're gonna be late for your flight, Patrice," Whisenhunt observed. "You'd better go. Best a' luck to you down there."

"Thanks, Richard," Patrice smiled. "There's no telling what we'll find but I'm sure we'll have our work cut out for us. This U.N. investigation has some of the world's best scientists on it." The lady doctor dug out a cigarette.

"I don't have any idea how I got on there," Thom added.

"Come now, you have every right to be included in that group," Whisenhunt chided.

Patrice whipped out her cigarette lighter and clicked several times, but no flame emerged.

"It doesn't work?" Whisenhunt stated the obvious. "You must know how important fire is in a jungle."

"Try this," Michael spoke up as he handed over his own lighter. "Keep it. I've been tryin' to cut back."

"Proud a' ya then," Whisenhunt chimed in. "Proud a' ya now." The statement elicited a smile from Michael.

"Thank you," Patrice grinned before lighting up and entering Flavortown.

"Well," the doctor spoke up. "You'd better go. Find out what's going wrong down there for us, eh?"

"Of course!" both Patrice and Thom said simultaneously.

"One a' you owe the other a Coke," Whisenhunt decreed by pointing.

Some time later, Dr. Whisenhunt and Michael stood out in the parking lot watching as a jet sped down the runway before lifting off into the air, taking Thom and Patrice onto a date with destiny. Whisenhunt waved as if they could be seen from the plane.

"Doctor," Michael started. "Maybe we should go soon. You have that, uh, appointment with that, um—"

"Oh, yeah, thanks!" Whisenhunt replied. "Let's get outta here." The two moved to enter the car with quick resolve.

Later, Dr. Whisenhunt had gone to a fellow pediatrician for a little con-fab. Dr. Laub was an older-looking man sitting behind a desk and with his all-white hair, looked as if he was late for retirement.

Whisenhunt looked through the x-rays of deformed fetuses through the light of a window. All had abnormalities. Some had cancerous growths. One had an extra head.

"According to a report we got from hospitals in northern California," Dr. Laub began. "A third of the babies born there are deformed or partially deformed.

A newborn only has a three-to-one chance of surviving. I've never seen anything like it in my life."

"Surely you aren't allowing them to live like this?" Whisenhunt inquired.

"When it's born," Laub began, "a fetus is already in a state of suffocation. For the most part, it's a matter of just allowing those ones to stay that way. Some might call it being still-born. I think it's a tragedy. One I'm helpless to prevent."

"But by not giving them a chance at life..." Whisenhunt haltingly thought aloud. "Aren't you killing them?"

"Are you calling me a murderer, Whisenhunt?" Laub asked in a sympathetic manner.

Whisenhunt, meanwhile, sat down to think on it. "In a way," he eventually began to speak. "I guess I am."

"I suppose then, that you'd allow them to survive?" Laub inferred. "Just as they are."

Whisenhunt really didn't have an answer for that. Dr. Laub stood up from behind his desk, then sat down in a chair across from Whisenhunt.

"Yeah, I know," Laub sighed. "It's a terrible situation, but I'm afraid we don't have any further recourse to help these babies at present. God knows I wish I did."

"Do you have *any* clue what's causing this?" Whisenhunt pressed.

"Nothing official," Laub shook his head. "But I think it's all those damned chemicals polluting the drinking water. That rocket fuel that was dumped into the water, and pharmaceutical drugs, if you remember some time back. And in places like Sierra Nevada, there's a lotta paper mills an' things like that. Mercury could have gotten into water supplies. All that stuff could easily have caused aberrations in the parents' genes."

"The families?" Whisenhunt asked as he scratched the back of his neck.

"God, what would you tell them?" Laub shot back. "I can't think of anything to ease the state of shock they're in when this happens."

"I hope this sort of thing doesn't spread across the U.S.," Whisenhunt said. Suddenly, he jerked back with surprise as he took note of something on the x-ray he was holding. One of the deformed fetus x-rays had the I.D. "*Sara Markham.*"

"What fresh hell is this?!?" Whisenhunt barked, grabbing Laub's attention anew. "Are you tellin' me that Sam's grandkid was one of these?!?"

"I guess..." Laub vacantly replied.

That evening, Jonathan and Phoebe were in the bedroom of their apartment getting dressed—readying themselves for a night out. Jonathan had been done at least ten minutes now and lay back on their bed, but Phoebe paced about, accessorizing herself. She was wearing a really expensive-looking ruby red textured cashmere sweater with a v-neck and dark blue slacks.

"Phoebes, are you sure you wanna do this?" Jonathan almost whined. "I mean, you know the doctor said you couldn't dance anymore."

"What're you saying??" Phoebe demanded to know as she attached an earring.

"Well, if you go watch this ballet," the young man explained. "You know you're going to wanna dance. And then you could do something even more serious to your leg."

"I wanna dance regardless of if I watch a ballet or not, ya knob," Phoebe fired back. "But since I can't anymore, I won't." She plopped down next to Jonathan, causing them both to rock up and down on the mattress. "Some of my girls are gonna be there tonight. What kinda teacher would I be if I didn't show up to support them? What kind of person would I be if I, a... former dancer... didn't support the ballet? Huh?" She stammered over that phrase "a former dancer."

Jonathan nodded his head. "Valid," he admitted. Phoebe smiled, then bent over and kissed Jonathan. She then got up and continued readying herself once more. Jonathan fell backward onto the bed in frustration. "No way out tonight, Jon" he mumbled to himself.

Later at Royce Hall, dancers participated in a ballet recital. Jonathan and Phoebe were in attendance. Some of the audience were enjoying what they were watching. Others—mostly the men—had checked out. Jonathan was bored to tears. Phoebe's attentions, however, were just shy of holding up a foam hand that read "We're #1!"

Bright colored lights flashed across the dancers on stage. It suddenly caused something to bother Jonathan. He grasped and clutched at his eyes before looking up at the stage again. On stage, the dancers en

masse moved into a pose and then equally en masse
shrunk down to six inches in height.

Jonathan's eyes bulged with equal parts
confusion and shock. Especially when he could've
sworn he heard the phrase "Mosura-ya, Mosura"
singing.

The dancers on stage returned to their normal
height and continued to dance as if nothing had actually happened—because it hadn't. Jonathan surely
couldn't tell that, though. Phoebe turned to look at
him and noticed his bewildered expression.

"Is something wrong?" she whispered.

Jonathan calmed down again but did not
answer. Phoebe looked him over one more time
before turning her attention back to the stage.

A train pulled to a stop at a station in a New
York City subway. The people inside the train exited,
while those waiting to board pushed their way inside.
Moments later, the train's doors closed and it pulled
away down the tracks.

Inside a subway car, some passengers chattered
endlessly as the train hauled them to their destinations.
There were some passengers keeping entirely to themselves.

In the engine room, the train's engineer sat
idly... until something in the distance caught his attention. The train's headlights lit up a massive amount of
weeds and vegetation collected ahead in the subway
tunnel. The engineer involuntarily gasped, then slammed on the brakes. Outside on the tracks, the subway

train itself collided through the massive weed growth. Slowly but surely, however, it came to a stop.

Passengers inside the train fell all over the place as the subway car screeched to a herky-jerky stop. When the confused patrons righted themselves, they recoiled with shock as they found the outside vegetation begin to move *inside* the train car of its own volition.

Elsewhere in a vacant area of the subway tunnels, sludge and vegetation pushed its way through a sewer tube and into the tunnel itself. In this tunnel, the weeds had managed to trap a subway train in its grasp like a spider with a fly.

Richard Whisenhunt had the attention of a bigwig government meeting in Washington D.C. The other government officials sat around an expansive table and seemed to be a collection of doughy, white men, except for Erica Cady, Madame President. She sat at the head of the table and wore a tan woman's business suit and matching male-style slacks.

"The vegetation appeared in New York subways overnight," Whisenhunt informed. "This unusual incident was one among many of the extraordinary phenomena occurring in America and there is no doubt that more such phenomena are yet to come. The people of Cleveland drank contaminated water from their city water system and all hell broke loose. A factory near the Rock and Roll Hall of Fame pumped dangerous amounts of lead, arsenic, and manganese into the water.

On a city sidewalk in Cleveland, Ohio, children milled about, presumably walking to school. An eight-year-old boy with shaggy brown hair walked extraordinarily fast, passing all the others in just several steps.

"Some of these infected children have developed amazing capabilities," Whisenhunt described the situation. "A few have discovered that they can walk with amazing speed."

Elsewhere in a Cleveland field, children had crowded around a young five-year-old girl. All of them stood before a four-rail fence that was easily over six feet tall. With a determined look on her face, the little girl made a run then suddenly leapt over the fence— and then some—before coming down, accompanied by the cheers of her peers.

"Others, like this little girl," the doctor explained to the others in the meeting, "have suddenly discovered that they can jump amazing heights. It seems that these capabilities are due to a distortion of the brain which can prove fatal later on in life. Indeed, many of the children there are already dying of complications. The affected parents do not seem to have abnormal abilities, but do act bizarre and erratic with anomalous brain patterns."

"So what would you have us do about it, Whisenhunt?" Kendell, an annoyed-looking, heavy-set senator inquired. "We are already trying to overcome our pollution problems with our most modern equipment. What more can we do?"

"Yes, I know you are, but who can say that your new modern equipment won't itself cause new problems?" the doctor postulated. "Already, exploitation of undersea oil fields has resulted in widespread pollution of the sea itself. Generation of electricity by terrestrial heat causes arsenic in the air. And look at nuclear energy: what do we do to dispose of the radioactive waste—"

"You've made your point, 'Doctor'—if you are, in fact, a doctor," Senator Selzner said in a haughty, snarky manner. He was an older career politician that just looked like he was bought off by special interests. "Civilization has reached a very developed state. We can't just go back. Progress is a human instinct. We have to keep moving on."

"And the Earth is littered with the ruins of cultures that had reached advanced levels of civilization," Whisenhunt responded, ignoring that jibe about his credentials. "Without exception, all of these civilizations have eventually failed and are nothing but stone monuments in a mountain somewhere. How can mankind presume to lord over the Earth? We make blind advancements and destroy the world around us. 'Advanced civilization'? What have we really accomplished?"

"But criticizing our current shortcomings does us no good," Avalon, a dark-skinned senator in a nice dark suit leaned forward. "We must develop for the future."

"Of course, science must look ahead," the doctor agreed. "But the developments you speak of will only result in one thing: the destruction of life on this planet."

"My opinion, Madame President?" Selzner interrupted as he held up his hand for attention.

"Yeeeees, go ahead," Cady almost sighed as if she knew what was coming.

"Whisenhunt, you're a misguided idealist," Selzner decreed. "We're going to solve our problems using scientific means. Your arguments are based on pure conjecture. You'd be better off sighting Nostradamus as evidence."

"He's right," Pfeiser, a younger senator that looked like it was his first term, agreed. "Aren't you supposed to be a scientist? Far as I can tell, you just spread panic with idle speculation. All this bullshit you use to keep disturbing the public. You are lying to them!"

"Now I'm a liar?" Whisenhunt rebuked with disdain in his voice. "If you think our pollution problems are a lie, perhaps you should go experience it for yourself. You may understand the concept academically but by the time you realize how it affects others, it's already too late. It may already be too late! I'm not alone in this line of thinking. Everything from the Bible to Nostradamus has predicted our societal problems today—the end of the age of reason has been creeping up on us for decades now! And all you lazy bastards have done is exacerbated it!"

Visibly incensed, some of the senators started to respond, but Cady cut them off. "Dr. Whisenhunt," Madame President began, leaning forward. "I appreciate your considered opinion. After all, you had the gall to punch Hannity on nationwide TV, so I know you're a smart guy. So tell me, please... if you were me, what do you think should be done? Let's hear what you have to say."

"Oh, this is gonna be good," Pfeiser rolled his eyes.

"To start with," Whisenhunt started himself, "work towards this end result for our citizens—giving people what they need: food, medicine, clean air, pure water, trees and grass, pleasant homes to live in, some hours of work, more hours of leisure. Many countries, even in the capitalist world, have strong social safety nets, universal and legally-required weeks or months off. And a two or three-hour post lunch period for napping every single day. These regulations are fading or being blocked from introduction here in the States because of lobbying, which is just plain ol' bribery at the end of the day."

"And just how would we determine who deserves that?" Selzner sneered.

"Don't ask who deserves it!" the doctor shot back. "Every human being deserves it!" Selzner just scoffed. "Do you have any idea how much shipping traffic would cut down if we switched to natural power sources?" Whisenhunt then rhetorically asked. "At least 75%. That's how much coal and oil we ship around the world at any given time. If we switched to solar and wind, that would cut down on the fuel spent on shipping drastically."

"But windmills kill the birds!" Kendell remarked.

"And cause cancer!" Pfeiser added.

"How the hell are you two in this building?" Whisenhunt again rhetorically asked.

"Gerrymandering," Cady deadpanned. "Now, Dr. Whisenhunt, what about nuclear energy? I've read that it's much cleaner than oil."

"It is," the doctor admitted, "but it's not practical. Do you know how long it takes to make a safe nuclear reactor and the plant to house it?" Silence answered him. "10 years," he continued. "We don't have that kind of time. We need solutions that will begin working for us now, not 10 years from now. That doesn't mean we shouldn't try them, but we can't just rely on them to solve our problems because they will get much worse before we can even start!"

"So what could we try?" Madame President respectfully inquired. "Can you recommend the best way to take action? It's not enough just to sit here and talk about it."

"There are great many things we could try," Whisenhunt answered. "But none of your associates here are gonna like any of it. The first thing you have to do is bar special interests from buying off the members of your government. Big Oil will drive this planet and everyone on it into the sun before it lets up on its profits."

Selzner scoffed derisively.

"But after that," the doctor continued, "we double down and end our reliance on fossil fuels. Oil and coal have to go."

"And what about all the people with jobs in those related fields?" Kendell said more than asked. "Do we just tell them 'Sorry, you're out of a job now'?"

"You re-train then re-hire them to work in the corresponding fields of the new power sources," Whisenhunt explained like it was the most natural thing in the world. "After that, we make greater energy efficiency. Make the paraphernalia around our energy consumptors last rather than need to be regularly replaced for company profits. Renewable energy, sustainable transportation—public and personal, sustainable buildings. Structures made to be energy-friendly. Better forestry management and sustainable agriculture. Take better care of our parks. We have them for a reason. We need conservation-based solutions, not profit-driven ones. Better industrial solutions that cut down on the air, water, and land pollution. There are entire rainforests we think of as 'ancient' and 'wild' that were essentially just immense gardens that provided people more food than they could even eat. Madame President, you would need to make an address to the American people. They have a right to know about the magnitude of these disasters among them. Let them know factually that in order to survive, they'll have to put up with all manner of discomforts. We'll close down some, no, all our fact-ories, except those that are essential for a period of at least ten years until pollution comes into check."

"What you're proposing is impossible!" Kendell balked loudly. Cady shifted her eyes from Whisenhunt to them and back to keep watch on how they respond-ed.

"Are you trying to collapse the economy even worse, Whisenhunt?!" Avalon questioned so angrily that his words nearly tripped over each other.

"Our survival has to take priority," Whisenhunt explained. "Everything will have to be reworked and food carefully rationed. We'll all have to learn to get by on much less. Develop a new diet. Perhaps we could even survive on wheat or grains alone, because we must check population growth."

"Alright, I've had enough a' yer socialist talk!" Selzner shouted.

"You can't do that!" Avalon fired back. "It goes against common decency!"

"Selzner's right!" Pfeiser put forth. "This is commie talk!"

"Saying such a thing belays your disconnection from reality!" Whisenhunt angrily replied. "Get outside and experience how horrible life is now! You've got to have the knowledge to actually come to terms with this crisis!"

"None of what you've said has become reality," Selzner observed.

"It will if you do nothing!" Whisenhunt bellowed. "You're too busy with your cheap-ass morality to realize the true size of this problem! You think I want my family putting up with this crap too? Hell no, I want them to be comfortable and happy... but comfortable and happy will not suffice if we're to solve this crisis! And *that's* why nobody wants to do anything!"

Chiang opened the door and charged into the room. He ran over to Cady and whispered into her ear.

"Aw, and it was just gettin' good," Cady grumbled as she rose to her feet. "I'm very sorry, but I'm needed elsewhere to make a statement. A jet airliner just crashed in Nevada because a flock of birds flew themselves into the engines. We'll convene this meeting until the summit next week. Thank you for your time and considered opinions. Dr. Whisenhunt, thank you very much." The president then turned and marched off.

Whisenhunt looked around at the smug, smirking senators before him. He quickly turned around and followed suit because if he hung around that room much longer, a fistfight likely would've broken out.

"Whackjob," Avalon scoffed.

"Another damn A.O.C.," Pfeiser mumbled.

"And we sure knew how to get rid a' her," Selzner stated. "We can deal with him too. If her majesty here doesn't get wind..."

The senators at the table nodded in agreement with themselves.

CHAPTER 6 - Abnormal Weather No Longer Abnormal

The skies over Egypt were dark and thunder rolled through them. But even worse was a blizzard, sprinkling snow through the air and across the sandy desert. On the ground, the Pyramids of Giza were capped with snow like a mountain. A group of Egyptians stood on their knees and prayed. Thunder boomed across the sky again.

The air of the Earth had become more and more polluted. Particles in the atmosphere were intercepting the sun's rays of light before they could even reach the Earth. As a result, the strength of the sun's rays had been weakened significantly.

The sun over the Pacific Ocean was being blocked by clouds of pollution in the air. Down below, a cargo ship did its best to make its way through the North Pacific because the Pacific Ocean, north of the Hawaiian Islands in the Subtropical Zone, had begun to freeze over.

On the ship, cold winds beat against the wheelhouse of the crew. The ship's captain, its first mate, and a few other crewmen were inside peering through the windows. The captain shook his head with disbelief. Out ahead of him as far as the eye could see was icy frozen slush that almost looked like one could walk over it. The ship was cutting its way through the slush with help from the engine, but cold winds still battered the vessel. Ice was hanging over the gunwale.

Because they were so busy trying to feel their way through this new version of the Pacific Ocean, the captain and his immediate crew were distracted enough that they never saw an iceberg floating through the sea toward them.

In the Gulf of Mexico, a change in the weather resulting in warm water, colder air, and high ambient humidity over the ocean had made a strange alteration. Waterspouts began to form between the surface of the sea and the clouds. But it wasn't just one; it could be as many as six at a time. When seen from a distance, they looked, moved, and behaved just like an army of tornadoes coming for the land.

Crews working on an oil rig in the Gulf looked out at them through binoculars.

"It's very common to see water spouts out here at certain times of the year," the captain stated. "But this many... at once? Call everybody in right now. Shut down the rig and bring everyone inside."

In Africa, native farmers tried desperately to find some kind of crops. There were none. A hungry goat dug into the ground in an attempt to kick up something edible.

In Southeast Asia, mothers and their babies were malnourished. Other less fortunate people lay in the gutters starving to death.

East Indians marched across an unusually barren India, carrying their meager belongings with them. Grain foodstuffs had to be rationed out to the citizenry.

Africa, India, and Southeast Asia all suffered from severe chronic droughts that ruined the harvest and pushed nearly a billion people to the brink of starvation.

After news of his stint in D.C. got around, Richard Whisenhunt became something of a minor media darling. His overall well-meaning crankiness became fodder for late-night comedians and detractors alike.

On one such talk show, Whisenhunt had been invited to give his unique perspective on the state of affairs of the environment to a nationwide audience. Phoebe and Europa cuddled up together on the couch in their living room to watch the live broadcast of the interview.

"So, what is it *really* like, Dr. Whisenhunt?" the show's early-middle-aged host queried. "Is there a way to dumb it down so idiots like me could understand?" The show's audience giggled.

"Hmm..." Whisenhunt mumbled as he rubbed his chin as he thought. "Let's try this thought experiment: you're trapped on a small submarine with ten other people deep under the ocean and the captain has had a heart attack."

"Okay..." the host warily kept up.

"The ballast system has clogged and you're slowly sinking," the doctor continued. "There's no communication with the topside world. The air is running out. Four passengers have already said they're feeling sick. The submarine is equipped with an emergency scuba tank that would give everyone another ten hours of fresh air. In fact, there's a technician on board who's sure she could use a small part of the pressure in the tank to clear the ballast line and start sending the whole sub toward the surface."

"Well, that sounds good," the host construed.

"Ah..." Whisenhunt replied, holding up his left index finger. "But one guy has stolen the oxygen tank and locked himself in the bathroom. He refuses to come out. He's even rigged the air vents so he gets cleaner air while everyone else's gets worse."

"What?!" the host acted like it was actually happening.

"You have about twenty minutes before the air is too toxic and everyone dies," Whisenhunt announced. "The guy locked in the bathroom will eventually die too... He'll just die last. What do you do?"

The host just looked around. The audience of the show gasped and looked around at each other.

Whisenhunt also looked around to see their reactions. "This is not just a thought experiment," he explained. "It's actually happening to us all right now. The submarine is the Earth and climate change is steadily destroying its ability to host life as we know it. The scuba tank is money. We could invest in some new technologies. We could reconfigure our economy and eliminate our dependence on fossil fuels. It would take a lot of money, willpower, and hard work but we *could* save our fragile little world if we tried. That guy in the bathroom? That's oligarchs and corporations who only care about themselves and extracting more money from the rest of us no matter the consequences. They don't want to change and they sure as hell don't want to share."

The host pulled away as if this was something that never occurred to him before.

"Back to the little submarine," Whisenhunt started again. "Now, there's just five minutes left. You have a raging headache from all the CO_2 in the air and slivers of frost cover the bulkheads as the sub sinks deeper and deeper. As it turns out, the door to the bathroom wasn't locked at all. It was just very hard to open. Now, what do you do?"

"I-I... I'm not sure," the host stammered.

"You bust open the door and eat that air-hording son of a bitch," Whisenhunt decreed. As the concept landed with the audience, they began to cheer and applaud. "If you want to live, that is," he continued. "Our dreams for the future aren't out of reach... they're just being held over our heads by the rich."

"But I'm rich and I'm not holdin' up anyone's dreams," the host defended.

"You aren't the obscene kind of rich we're talking about," Whisenhunt stated, dead seriously.

"Yikes..." the host barely got out.

Whisenhunt nodded. "I think corporations," he began again, "or at least the people making the decisions, should be held accountable for environmental issues at the severity level that we treat traitors to military intelligence. Destroying the country physically should be taken as seriously as national security at this point. Risking lives and poisoning the land, animals, and air of our nation should not be something a corporation can just pay a fine on and move on from."

"I don't think our corporate overlords would appreciate that," the host spoke through an uncomfortable grin.

"That they wouldn't," Whisenhunt agreed.

On another occasion, a young-ish male reporter came out to Whisenhunt's home to interview him for an article for *The Los Angeles Daily News*. As Europa was home at the time, she participated as well and dressed up in a nice dark blue dress that made her look like she was going to a funeral for the occasion. The reporter listened intently as Whisenhunt spoke.

"...People used to be able to feed their family on what they found in what was practically their own backyard," the doctor espoused. "Some people still manage to do it if the local ecosystem is healthy enough. You can still live entirely on netting your own fish in some parts of the world with only a, uh... 'minimal' risk of mercury poisoning." He made an ironic facial expression as he said the last bit. "Human beings all over the world suffer from dwindling or already lost resources that should not be dwindling and never dwindled before the sloppy, wasteful methods of modern 'profitable' business."

The reporter scribbled down every word. "How have you reacted to the media's... well, let's say embellishment of your demeanor, sir?" the reporter changed the subject.

Whisenhunt shrugged as he thought. "They're gonna do what they do," he replied. "I have no control over it, so why worry about it? I've got bigger things on my plate."

"Can I say something?" Europa spoke up.

"By all means, do," the reporter answered.

"He's only like that maybe two hours a day at most," Europa began. "There's 24 hours in a day. He's been trying to warn you about this stuff since the '40s—and probably before—and nobody ever listens. That's bound to make anyone impatient and grouchy. But that's not all he is."

"If he's been seeing this coming since then," the reporter thought as he spoke. "Does that make him a new Nostradamus?"

"He is *not* Nostradamus," Europa curtly shot back. "He just pays attention better than most. Sees the signs and knows the science. And he's not alone in all this. Go talk to Nishiyama in Japan or Radeau in France."

Out of nowhere, Europa began to have a coughing fit. The reporter pulled back away from her as she doubled over and squinted her eyes shut as coughs just fired on repeat out of her mouth.

"Europa?" Whisenhunt called out as he gently beat her back with the palm of his hand.

Finally, Europa stopped coughing and sat back up on her own. "Sorry about that," she weakly said.

"It's quite... quite alright," the reporter replied.

"Guess something really went down the wrong pipe," she waved it off. Whisenhunt couldn't stop looking at his wife and Europa took note. "What??" she balked. "I'm alright now."

Back in D.C., Whisenhunt had the floor of the president's environmental summit. Madame President sat at the head of the table while each side was flanked by government big-wigs. Many of the underlings in the room were not happy with the sort of press Whisenhunt had been getting or how he'd been portraying them to the media. He wasn't doing so inaccurately, but they still didn't like it.

"Indigenous Hawaiian koi farms," the doctor explained, "fed a whole community and demanded only 20 hours of labor a month from their tenders. Most of these farms were destroyed by American imperialists and environmental degradation, though some are still around and are being looked to as models for climate-friendly agricultural solutions."

Cady nodded her head. Some of the others just looked bored, though, but Whisenhunt still had most of the room's attention.

"Mesoamerican agriculture," he continued, "such as the chinampa in Mexico are similarly effective, using lakes to grow semi-aquatic crops that support local biodiversity and, in turn, more food. In fact, axolotls were once plentiful enough to be a food source there. Today, they're very nearly extinct in their last heavily-polluted habitat."

"Uh, what is an 'axolotl'?" one older-middle-aged man in a grey suit inquired.

"It's, uh..." Whisehunt thought aloud. "It's like an aquatic salamander."

"I felt better when I didn't know," the grey-suited man muttered under his breath.

"There is a conflict beginning to rapidly develop between the industrialized and underdeveloped nations that are only being aggravated by the world food crisis," the doctor explained as he passed data around the table. "Take the Japanese islands and how much food they supply domestic, for example: it's 40%. This proportion is one of the world's lowest. What will happen to those people with a worldwide food shortage when they can't import the 60% they need? Maybe it won't happen this year or even the next, but it will eventually happen."

"You've made a good point, Dr. Whisenhunt," Cady acknowledged as she looked over his data. "The damage has been done and like others, we're aware of the crisis. A few of my people are drawing up a new food program, designed to promote self-sufficiency. At this moment, it's in the late development stages. I'm going to recommend to our Japanese friends that they do they same."

"That's good," Whisenhunt yielded. "But can you turn a barren field into fertile land overnight? You can't. And will the youth that left the country to work in the cities come back? What are you gonna do, order them back? Adults can't order young people to do jack."

"I'm aware of that too," Madame President sighed. "You're right, this will take some time to solve. Thank you, gentlemen, that is all. We've got to succeed at all costs. There is no room for failure."

"But Madame President," Whisenhunt pressed. "I'm asking exactly how you plan to make them work?" Cady glared up at him for demanding answers she didn't have.

"Excuse me a moment!" Jergens interrupted as he stood up. "The U.N. Investigation team that went to investigate the strange phenomena in Madagascar have all disappeared."

"What? How??" Cady demanded to know. Other people in the room began to murmur amongst themselves. Whisenhunt was visibly taken aback by this turn of events.

"The aforementioned phenomena occurring in Madagascar," Jergens explained, "is thought to have been caused by radioactive dust clouds gathering over the island, but the cause of the dust clouds to gather there is unknown. The United Nations want to send in a second party to investigate and rescue the first team, if they are still alive."

"Get me on that team, Madame President," Whisenhunt respectfully insisted.

That night in the Whisenhunt kitchen back in Los Angeles, Richard, Phoebe, and Jonathan sat around the table with a farewell dinner spread out before them. The couple listened at attention as the doctor recounted the day's events.

"Everyone is stressed beyond endurance with the collective knowledge of our imminent demise and the effects of unchecked capitalism on a planet over-populated by a species hell-bent on self-destruction and the people who might be able to do something about it don't even really care," he stated. Phoebe and Jonathan looked ahead, wide-eyed, unable to even blink. "But don't worry, it's gonna get worse, before it gets worse," the doctor sighed.

"Worse-er," Europa erroneously corrected as she entered the kitchen. She sat down next to her husband, then began to reach for something to eat, but her husband stopped her.

"I think that we should have a prayer before this meal," Whisenhunt softly said.

"You're right," Europa agreed. "That's probably a good idea."

Phoebe nudged Jonathan in his ribs, causing him to set down a chicken leg he was about to chomp into. Everyone bowed their heads. Europa and Phoebe crossed the fingers of their hands into the Namaste gesture.

"Oh, Heavenly father," Whisenhunt began. "Bless this home and all who dwell within it. We thank you for this meal which we are about to receive. We also want to send our thoughts and well-wishes to the U.N. team in Madagascar... Amen."

"Amen," the rest parroted en masse. At that point, everyone began grabbing for various foodstuffs and started eating dinner.

"Are you really going all that way to go look for them?" Europa inquired.

"Who?" her husband absent-mindedly answered her question with a question.

"That lost U.N team," Europa said with a cough.

"I have to," Whisenhunt responded between bites of chicken. "Some of those people on that team are friends of mine. Friends don't leave friends in the lurch."

"When do you have to leave?" Phoebe asked as she ate.

"Tuesday," her father replied.

"Tuesday's gonna come up on us fast," Europa thought aloud.

"Yeah... tomorrow, Mom," Phoebe retorted.

"Tomorrow?!" Europa shot back with a heavy breath like it hadn't occurred to her. "Sonuvabitch!"

"You mind if I tag along, Doc?" Jonathan spoke up. "I didn't get a chance to go into Madagascar last time I was over there."

"I got a plus one. You're quite welcome, Jonathan," the doctor answered.

"Hey, whaddaya think you're doing?!" Phoebe demanded to know. "Are you trying to steal my boyfriend away from me?" Whisenhunt shrugged and made facial reactions like "Yeah, maybe."

"Don't be silly, Phoebe," Europa said. "Jonathan could make some good money getting some great photos down there. Your dad's right. Even though it may be dangerous down there, they have to find out what's going on. Imagine if Jonathan were to win a Pulitzer because of some amazing photo he takes. You two would be set for the rest of your lives."

"Well, I'm not that good," the young man fidgeted.

"Nonsense," Europa responded before succumbing to a sudden coughing fit. Whisenhunt leaned over to her level, but she waved away help from her husband. Phoebe and Jonathan just watched.

"Europa, you alright?" Whisenhunt asked loudly over the coughing just as it finally stopped.

"Yes, I'm okay," Europa answered. "Something just went down the wrong pipe is all." Whisenhunt watched his wife uncomfortably because she obviously didn't remember she'd already made that excuse once before.

CHAPTER 7 - Madagascar

A jet zoomed down the runway of LAX International and rose into the sky. From a parking lot in the distance, Europa and Phoebe watched sitting on the back of their Equinox, waving at the jet as if its passengers could see them.

Inside the jet, Dr. Whisenhunt was sitting in a window seat. He looked outside anxiously as he saw the ocean below. From his vantage point, he could see piles and piles of garbage floating on top of the sea, being drifted about by the ocean currents.

"*How did we even let it come to this?*" he thought to himself.

Over a day later—28 hours, to be exact—the flight from Los Angeles made it to the Fascene Airport in Nosy Be, Madagascar. The jet came in for a landing on a much smaller airfield than it had left. Some native Malagasay peoples stood by, watching. They waved in greeting to the plane as it landed.

After they had disembarked and got through customs at the airport, Whisenhunt and Jonathan approached another group of scientists waiting for them already. A tall British man reading a newspaper was sitting in a lobby chair. He peered out from behind the paper and Whisenhunt saw him.

"Dr. Cole?" the doctor inquired.

The tall scientist put his paper away to turn his full attention toward the rest of his party. He was indeed Dr. Ford Cole. Lanky and immaculately dressed in a white suit with a Burt Reynolds-like mustache.

"A pleasure to meet you, Dr. Whisenhunt. We've been waiting for you."

"Well, you know," Whisenhunt began. "Government flights. Ya get what ya paid for."

"Quite," Cole offered. "Come. Let's introduce you to the rest of our little group," he said as the three began to walk away. "Who is your friend here, Doctor?"

In the town of Andoany, its townsfolk milled about the place. A couple of jeeps carrying the second U.N. team made its way down the town's roads. Whisenhunt and Jonathan sat in the back of the jeep, taking note of the town around them as they advanced. Jonathan carefully aimed his camera and snapped off a picture of Whisenhunt.

"You know," the young man began as he looked over his camera. "Did they tell you this town used to be known as 'Hell-Ville'?"

"No, they neglected to mention that little tidbit," Whisenhunt responded.

Outside, the convoy of jeeps made its way down the roads. Walking native Malagasays moved to the side of the road to let the jeeps pass.

Whisenhunt fanned himself with a white Panama Jack hat. Jonathan snapped off photographs of his surroundings through the windows.

"Driver?" the doctor spoke up. "Are we going that way?"

"Yessuh," the jeep's driver replied.

Out in the forest-laden countryside, massive cloud covers blanketed the area. It was a weird silvery color that did not look natural in the least.

Meanwhile, back on the ground, the jeep convoy passed over the water of a shallow river. A water buffalo watched tacitly as the vehicles passed by.

Later, the U.N. team had made its way into a jungle topped with Baobabs trees and had to proceed on foot, with a trio of native Malagasay guides on hand. The team was entirely surrounded by vegetation that gave it a rain forest feel. The three guides hacked their way through the foliage with machetes. The sun above rained blistering light down upon them.

Even later still, the team was dressed in hazmat suits. Geiger counters being carried went off all around. The team studied everything around them as they advanced. The noise of a squawking bird got their attention. Everyone turned en masse just in time to see a poor sickle-billed vanga dragged into the middle of a large colorful flower, whose petals closed over it, trapping it inside. The team rushed up to the plant while Jonathan snapped off photographs.

"Look at this!" a scientist exclaimed. "I'd never imagined a plant like that could even exist!"

"It's probably some kind of mutation," Dr. Cole surmised.

"Figures," Whisenhunt deadpanned. "My guess would be because of the radioactivity."

"Quite," Cole agreed with a grin.

Even later, the team sloshed their hazmat boots through a shallow creek that was somehow even deeper than the river they passed through. Geiger counters continued to buzz. But after continuing their trek for a while, the counters suddenly went off. One of the scientists took note. "I think we can take off these suits now."

The team pulled off their helmets. Jonathan shook his hair free. Whisenhunt took a deep breath of air.

"Christ All-Friday, those things are hard to breathe in," the doctor observed.

"I never thought I'd have to wear one of these things in Madagascar," Dr. Shaan, a bespectacled Indian scientist, spoke up with an accent.

Out of nowhere, a bat shrilled nearby, grabbing the team's attention. Suddenly, a swarm of gigantic eagle-sized Madagascar Flying Foxes began to dive bomb the team, presumably for food. Some of the scientists gasped with shock.

"Get down!" one called out. "Get down!"

A flying fox passed over the team and they ducked to avoid it. Other bat-foxes followed, some flying about, others just passing over the team. Jonathan tried to snap a photo, but was nearly hit by one of the flying foxes who did not care about how much bigger he was at all.

"Let's get outta here!" one of the scientists shouted.

"No, stay down!" Whisenhunt shot back.

Apparently not listening, one of the Malagasay guides swung for the fences with their machete and managed to not only hit one of the bat-foxes, but slice its right wing off.

Jonathan jerked out of the way of an incoming flying fox. Whisenhunt rolled out of the way as one passed. The flying foxes continued their assault. Cole grabbed a thick, sturdy tree limb, then jumped to his feet and whacked a bat out of the sky. It hit the ground with a shriek.

Dr. Shaan pulled a pistol and started shooting. Several of the flying foxes went limp and fell out of the sky. After a few moments, the remaining fox-bats were gone or dead. The team cautiously rose back to its feet.

One member kicked a downed flying fox's corpse. Its head and face looked strangely lupine rather than like a bat.

"Jonathan, are you alright, my boy?" Cole questioned with legitimate concern in his British voice.

"I'm okay, just a little jarred," the young man reported.

"The small animals they generally feed upon have been annihilated," Whisenhunt made an educated guess. "They've been forced to go after larger prey... Us."

Suddenly, Dr. Shaan groaned with pain causing the others to rush over to him.

"Is that an ant?!" Jonathan incredulously asked.

A gigantic frog-sized Dracula ant had gotten onto Dr. Shaan and bitten into his neck. Whisenhunt whipped out a small knife and used the blade to peel the giant ant out of Shaan's neck. Once free, he deftly flung it to the ground. Dr. Cole snatched Shaan's pistol off the ground and fired a shot, blowing the Dracula ant to kingdom come in a shattered blast of exoskeleton and blood.

Out of nowhere, water began to pour down upon the team. Whisenhunt touched some with his hand and rubbed his fingers together. "Acid rain!" he gasped.

"C'mon, let's get outta here!" a scientist yelled. Sure enough, the team ran for cover as discolored water rained down upon them. Whisenhunt and Cole helped the groaning Dr. Shaan along the way. Some of the team members had put their hazmat helmets back on.

"Get a blood transfusion ready for him!" Whisenhunt shouted to the team.

As the team advanced under a canopy of trees to get in out of the acid rain, Jonathan barely noticed something shiny on the ground. He snatched it up as he moved along and looked it over. It was a cigarette lighter.

"*What's a cigarette lighter doing all the way out here?*" he questioned himself. But he failed to notice the lighter looked an awfully lot like the one given to Patrice Sherman before she left L.A.

CHAPTER 8 - Living Hell

By nightfall, the U.N. team had found a docile part of the jungle to set up base camp and erected three large tents for the members to stay in. While the three Malagasay guides helped put up the tents, by now they had left for who knows where, but promised they would return.

Inside the one closest to the surrounding forest, Dr. Shaan had been placed on a cot and was in the middle of receiving a blood transfusion as Dr. Whisenhunt had prescribed. Dr. Cole was tending to his colleague as best he could. The other members of the team were all huddled in close by out of genuine care.

"That Dracula ant that bit him probably fed on the blood of animals contaminated by radiation or God knows what else," Whisenhunt thought aloud, as he gently shook a glass of whiskey. "Could have even contaminated its nest. Certainly that thing was much larger than they should be."

"Then, you mean to say," another scientist began, "those giant bats that attacked us... ?"

"Were probably contaminated by strong radioactivity as well," Whisenhunt sighed and took a drink.

Shaan groaned but did not move.

"And Shaan's been wounded..." a scientist almost whined. The others all moved closer to the prone scientist.

Cole slowly looked over at them. "I'm doing the best I can," he explained. "But I'm not sure that he'll live."

"Did all the members of that first research team die like this?" Jonathan put forth.

No one had time to answer or even think about it as Dr. Shaan slowly sat up, his upper body stock-still and his face just glazed over into a nothing expression.

"Shaan??" Cole called out. "Are you alright, Dr. Shaan?"

Shaan's head slowly turned to Cole and as if the flip of a switch, began yelling, then getting out of the cot, raving like a lunatic, and smashing things about in the tent. Some scientists ducked out of the way, all yelling to look out. Whisenhunt leapt forth and tackled Shaan to the ground. Others grabbed hold of Shaan and tried to pull him back to his feet. The frenzied scientist threw one of them off with a judo throw.

The others in the team grabbed him at once, then managed to pull him off his feet and set him back down in his cot. Shaan once more tried to get away in a fit of madness, but the others held him down. As if the flick of another switch, Shaan suddenly went quiet and calmed down again. Dr. Cole nervously held his hand out to feel Shaan's forehead.

"There's some kind of brain damage here," the Brit ascertained. "One moment, he's in an unruly rage, the next he's docile as a kitten."

Whisenhunt slowly raised up the lighter that Jonathan had found, then flicked its flame on. He looked off in dejection as he realized whose it was and how it got there.

Rustling noises outside pulled his attention back to the present. The U.N. team snapped into action, breaking out a footlocker of rifles and distributing them amongst the others.

"Should we get our suits?" a scientist queried.

"Nah, not in this area," another answered while checking over their rifle.

The team members exited the tent, looking about the darkened jungle, rifles armed and at the ready.

"I wonder what that sound was?" a scientist muttered aloud.

Out in the jungle before them, rustling could not only be heard but also seen. There was definitely something moving around out there but it was just too dank and dark to make anything out.

Clanging noises from inside the tent grabbed Whisenhunt, Cole, and Jonathan's attention. They turned and headed back into the tent. As the trio entered, they looked around, then jerked back with shock, bumping into the others. Two strange apparently native men were bent over the prone Shaan's body making odd slurping noises.

"Hey, shoo!" Whisenhunt shouted. "Get the hell outta here!"

The two slowly turned around, revealing themselves to be a duo of grungy-looking men. But far more importantly, they had blood and viscera dripping from their mouths. Their faces were badly scarred with burn marks and both had the disposition of wild animals.

Whisenhunt couldn't believe what he was seeing: a hole had been torn—or chewed—into the now deceased Dr. Shaan's body. The two animal-men were pulling anything they could get out of the body and devouring it. Jonathan tried to turn around to vomit, but one of the wild men suddenly rushed Whisenhunt, getting his attention back again. Dr. Cole promptly shot the charging wild man, followed by the second. The two cannibals fell to the ground, dead.

"Dr. Shaan!" Cole yelled in vain as he rushed over to the Indian scientist's corpse. "Dr. Shaan...!"

Dr. Whisenhunt and Jonathan exited the tent. Jonathan wearily wiped away his mouth with visible revolt.

"Be on your guard, gentlemen..." Whisenhunt warned. "We are not alone. They may be who we—"

Out of nowhere, more madmen jumped out of nowhere and attacked the team. They made unnerving screaming noises as they hopped about, which succeeded in discombobulating everyone. One of them grabbed Whisenhunt and hurled him to the ground. Another managed to pick up Jonathan around his groin and chest and tossed him away. The young man grunted as he hit the ground hard. As he rolled onto his back, another madman tried to jump onto him to attack, but Jonathan knocked him away with a solid right punch to the jaw.

Some members of the team were trying to keep the attackers off them while others took aim with their rifles. Dr. Cole managed to fire off a shot, knocking one of the madmen from his colleague. Another scientist got off a shot, killing his target.

The wild man that grabbed Whisenhunt was still wrestling with him on the ground. The doctor did his best to keep the madman's mouth at bay. "Stop firing!" he shouted. "Don't kill them! We came to save these people!"

The wild man tried to take a bite of Whisenhunt's arm, but Jonathan rushed in and knocked him away. He grabbed the doctor's targeted arm and pulled him to his feet to join the rest of the team.

"Look!" a scientist pointed.

More mad wild men jumped seemingly out of nowhere. They had burns and open sores looking like radiation scars on their faces, hands, and other parts of their bodies. They were not the same type of person—they were varying races and body types. Some were completely naked while others still had scraps of clothing hanging from them. This was what had eventually become of the original United Nations investigation team.

One scientist took aim with a rifle and blew a wild man away. Several more shots rang out and more madmen went down. Whisenhunt exasperatingly threw up his arms in resignation. Even he realized all bets were off.

The remaining wild men finally got the picture and turned to run off like scared rabbits.

"Let's go after them!" a scientist suggested. "Maybe we can find some other surviving members of the research party!"

"Should we wait for the guides?" Jonathan tried to push some logic into the situation.

"No telling when they'll be back," Cole countered. "If we're gonna go, best if we go now."

As if in tune with each other, the team headed out, passing over the corpses of the madmen at their campsite.

The U.N. team made their way through the jungle armed with guns and flashlights. Where they thought they were going was anyone's guess. It would have been impossible to know where they even were without their guides. That didn't seem to deter them any, though. They started splashing through a shallow creek, looking about and carefully watching for further attackers out there.

Eventually, the team came upon a cave near the stream. They all congregated at its mouth and looked about. Whisenhunt turned around to make sure nothing was behind them.

"It's a cave!" Cole stated the obvious.

"Look here," another scientist spoke up. "There are some tracks leading out of the stream and into the cave."

"Okay... let's go," Cole whispered. "Be careful."

Jonathan looked over at Whisenhunt. The doctor just shrugged his shoulders before the two followed.

The team entered the cave warily. It was dark and dank and water seeped in from above. The only spots that were visible were those where the flashlights shone. One such flashlight ray came upon a rotting human skeleton just laying there. Most members of the team gasped as they realized what it was. Cole moved his own flashlight about and found a few more rotting skeletons nearby.

"Dinner," the Brit surmised with an ill look on his face.

"How many are there?" Jonathan asked.

"Hard to say," a scientist sighed. "You can't tell whose bones these are."

Whisenhunt spied something on the ground and picked it up. He pointed his own flashlight at it to investigate. "Look," he muttered. "This is part of their uniform."

The team pressed further on into the darkness. All they could see as they advanced were mud and dirt and edges of the cavern walls. After a while, they came upon more of the wild madmen seen at the camp lining the walls of the cave. Each one sat staring straight ahead in some mix of consciousness and zombification.

The team threw their flashlights on the men's faces, eliciting no reaction from any of them. They moved over to the nearest one.

"Doctor?" Cole called out. "Doctor??" The man was still unresponsive.

Another scientist approached another of the wild men. "Professor!" the scientist said. "Professor Garnackle! It's me! Don't you see me?!" The scientist shook the body of the man that used to be Garnackle... the flesh slid right off the arm revealing bone inside the rather dry-looking grue.

Whisenhunt scanned the visible men as best he could. He stopped as someone else caught his attention: Patrice Sherman. Her once lovely face was scarred with radiation burns.

Reacting just short of a blue screen of death, Whisenhunt slowly walked over to her position. As he looked over her body, he found a bloated stomach that looked an awful lot like pregnancy. He also spied his lab assistant Thom huddled against her. The doctor was not only speechless but thoughtless as well. He could not comprehend what he was seeing, or at least was in utter denial of it.

Cole took aim with Dr. Shaan's pistol and prepared to open fire, but Jonathan leapt in and stopped him.

"What the hell're you doing?!" the young man demanded to know, his raised voice echoing through the cave.

Dr. Cole looked over at Jonathan, doing his best to keep his British stiff upper lip, but pretty obviously on the verge of tears. "There's nothing we can do for them," he intoned. "Their minds are gone. Have you a better idea? We should like to hear it."

Whisenhunt was still studying Patrice. With the blink of his eyes, he suddenly became active again, moving over and snatching the gun away from Cole. Everyone just stood by watching. The doctor slowly took aim with the gun, then paused a moment. He took a breath and then pulled the trigger, blowing Patrice's brains all over the cavern wall. He lowered the gun and fired one more time, doing the same for Thom.

The doctor held out the gun for Cole to take back. As soon as the firearm was out of his grasp, Whisenhunt ran for the exit of the cave. Jonathan closed his eyes and turned away as his mind broke.

Managing to make it to the cave's mouth, Dr. Whisenhunt staggered out into the stream, himself in a zombie-like gait. Out of nowhere, more gunshots rang out from within. They frightened Whisenhunt into moving further away, over to grab hold of the nearest tree for comfort.

There were more and more gunshots. Each shot echoed out of the cavern. Cole slowly emerged from within the mouth. He staggered up behind Whisenhunt and put his hand on his left shoulder.

"They couldn't be helped," Cole whispered in a low voice. "They're better off now... They're with God."

"'God'... ?" Whisenhunt parroted with some mix of hurt and disdain in his voice. "Why would God let such hell on Earth happen? Especially to people that did nothing to deserve it?" Cole nodded his head as he staggered away. "And if this atrocious thing can happen here..." the traumatized doctor continued. "Then who's to say that tomorrow, the rest of the world won't be in hell?"

Early the next morning, the sun's rays wafted through the jungle. Nobody on the team got any rest as they were up all night digging graves and carrying corpses. The three guides managed to return, forlorn that they had not helped in what had gone on in the night.

The team was currently in the middle of a mass funeral. The ground around them was littered with raised dirt, a grave for each of the dead U.N. team members. This reconnaissance team stood by with bowed heads, except for one of the scientists doing his best to officiate a service.

"The Lord is my Shepherd," the scientist shakily decreed. "I shall not want. He maketh me to lie down in green pastures. He leadeth me beside the still waters. He restoreth my soul. He leadeth me in the paths of righteousness for His name's sake... Yea, though I walk through the valley of the shadow of death, I will fear no evil, for thou art with me..."

Whisenhunt and Jonathan stood morosely over what was Patrice and Thom's graves. The doctor was not at all interested in hearing where the Lord leadeth anyone. In fact, there was only one thought that kept echoing through his mind:

"Who's to say that tomorrow, the rest of the world won't be in hell... ? "

CHAPTER 9 - The End Times Are Comin'

Some time later, a supersonic jet zoomed off a runway into the sky in Seattle. The beginning of its voyage was smooth sailing, but about a half hour into the flight, the pilots could tell something was off about their jet. The metal under one of the wings was bubbling from a heating error. It did not take long for the jet to explode in midair.

"We've just received word that a supersonic jet accidentally exploded this afternoon at a quarter to one while flying over Washington state," news anchor Lee Silliman stated for his viewers.

On a rooftop in Seattle, a group of young girls played a game of kickball. Without warning, the sky flashed brightly and the girls suddenly began to shriek and instinctively ran for the nearest door to the building. Once inside, as the girls tried to run down the stairs away from the roof, they screamed and sobbed uncontrollably. Radioactivity burns had charred themselves into the exposed skin of their faces and hands.

"People should stay inside," Silliman advised. "Do not leave your houses. The jet exploded in the skies over Seattle at a quarter to one this afternoon and things have gotten steadily worse ever since."

Lee Silliman sat behind a news desk in the TV studio speaking to the camera filming him. Lee was a thin, middle-aged man with neat, short black hair that was beginning to bald. He wore glasses that made him appear wiser for the viewing audience.

"The reason is still not clear," Silliman continued, "but sabotage has been ruled out. The explosion has affected the Ozone Layer in that area. Nitrous Oxide has accumulated in the atmosphere and ultraviolet rays are now hitting the Earth."

In Seattle, hanging vines growing up the side of a building were being buffeted by the sun's rays. The vines suddenly began to wilt away from burn damage.

Out in a Washington countryside near Mount St. Helens, the sun's rays shone down upon a series of rolling hills. It did not take long for the foliage growing there to burn away, leaving nothing but charred hillside behind. Dirt began to roll with the wind. Rocks under the ground began to steam. The landscape became nothing but a plantless void.

In the vicinity, the front door of a country house swung open and a family of four—the father, mother, daughter, and a brother—ran from the home, screaming. As soon as they got outside, the sun's rays hit them and caused them to almost immediately fall to the ground writhing in pain.

"I'm burning!" the little girl cried out, but her family could offer no respite. Their clothes and skin began to burn and char with them in it. Behind them, the roof of their house caught fire.

Elsewhere, the whole countryside spontaneously combusted into a great fireball. What remained of what was once a forest burned away at an alarming rate.

In Puget Sound Harbor that night, the heat got to an oil tanker currently docked and caused it to explode right there at the shoreline. The explosion hit the nearby oil refinery to which the ship had brought its cargo and caused it to explode as well. Licks of orange danced into the night sky as the whole Seattle shoreline burst into flame. People scattered and evacuated in terror as all hell broke loose.

Several more ships blew up as the fires raged uncontrollably. Dock workers tried to escape with their lives. Smoke began to cloak the immediate area like an umbrella.

In the TV studio, Lee Silliman reported the disasters as footage of the explosions played on a monitor behind him. "A fire in Puget Sound caused by an explosion of oil tanks is raging uncontrollably, despite all efforts to squelch it," he explained. Lee pulled back as a member of the news crew spoke into his earpiece. "This just in," he uneasily began. "A North Korean nuclear missile was fired and exploded above the Arctic Ocean and the Earth's protective Ozone Layer is slowly being destroyed. If the ultraviolet rays continue to strike the Earth, there may be more atmospheric disasters." Silliman looked over at people off camera. "What?" he incredulously whispered. "Is this right? Did that moron over there really do that?"

In the arctic region, massive amounts of what remained of the glacial material broke off and floated away. Pieces of ice fell off like cake crumbs and splashed into the ocean.

"The destruction of the Ozone in the stratosphere has caused a drastic change in the Earth's weather and distribution of atmospheric pressure," Silliman continued his staunch reporting.

On the remaining ice, helpless polar bears tried to flee the crumbling shoreline of their icy home.

In the sky over Miami, Florida, dark clouds moved into position and blocked out the sun. Thunder and lightning struck and a heavy storm began to pour down on the metropolitan city below. For days and nights, the rain poured down hard onto the city. People caught in the storm scrambled to get in behind doors.

"The great heat has caused a large-scale heat wave," Silliman explained. "As a result, warm air is being sucked up from the south, clashing with the colder air and creating violent storms such as those in Miami. The weather bureau has announced..."

People stuck out in the storm watched and waited for the rain to disappear. However, from the looks of things, it seemed to be getting much worse.

Water from the Atlantic crashed against the shores of the city and it didn't take long for it to splash up over the shoreline.

A rush of floodwaters crashed over the side of a mountain in a countryside grassland, eroding dirt away in a massive landslide. The stream of water rushed over the ground as though a dam had bust.

Cars zoomed dangerously fast over a bridge, trying to beat the oncoming torrent. The water rushed past and overtook the bridge, overturning the passing cars unfortunate to be caught still there. In no time, nothing but water could be seen in the area.

Nearby, a young couple sat in their home watching television and chewing on a snack. The rain outside continued to pour down and the water made its way toward the comparatively small house. The walls did not stop the water from crashing through and overtaking the shocked couple, washing them away from their couch. The tide of water completely destroyed the house in a matter of seconds.

As a result of floodwaters, cars sat half-submerged in water. Gas pumps had water standing at their feet. Survivors weakly made their way through the water in rowboats. In neighborhoods, only the roofs of houses stuck up out of the surface of the water.

"Another news flash," Lee Silliman announced for the public. "The Mississippi River has flooded its banks. It appears to be the worst in American history. The whole Green Crop area has been destroyed. And the Great Lakes have also overflowed, destroying the Wheat Belt."

A crowd of people stood on the banks of a river watching as the river itself burned with fire as if the water itself were gasoline. Firefighters on the scene tried futilely to extinguish the flames with their spray hoses.

Some onlookers watched with amazement. Others looked upon this with a dire sense of dread. The flames began to spread out and some of the crowd was forced backward. A partially burning tree toppled over and splashed into the liquid inferno.

In the TV studio, Lee Silliman was once again behind the news desk to report the day's disasters. "This afternoon in Iowa," he began. "A river suddenly erupted into a fire which has so far proved inextinguishable. Experts are attributing this bizarre occurrence to the inordinately high level of pollutants and trash dumped within the river's waters. Elsewhere, in the Ukraine, there have been an unusually high temperatures and a drought has ruined their harvest. The same thing has happened in Australia. All the major wheat-producing countries have been severely affected by the rise in temperatures."

While the men were off on their Madagascar nightmare vacation, Europa Whisenhunt had been diagnosed with leukemia as a result of exposure to benzene pollutants in the air—the handiwork of factories her husband had previously been trying to have shut down or curtailed. She had been relocated to Phoebe and Jonathan's apartment so she wouldn't be left alone so much and Phoebe could look out for her. Her natural black hair color was beginning to seep through her blonde dye. Today, Europa was lying on the couch in the living room, watching Silliman deliver the news on television. She was covered in heavy blankets. She coughed uncontrollably.

"The country of Japan has been placed in a perilous situation," the anchor explained more bad news, "as they import all of their food and supplies are no longer there. They appear to be on their own."

Phoebe entered and turned off the TV.

"It's all terrible," Europa weakly sighed. "It's just like your father said would happen, Phoebe. This is the only time I wish that he was wrong. Well, not the only time, but especially now."

Phoebe sat down on her knees next to her mother on the couch. "He should have come back home by now," she said. "Why isn't he more worried about you, Mom?"

"It's alright," Europa waved her off. "His message getting out is far and away more important than little ol' me." She punctuated that with another uncontrollable coughing fit.

"Mom!" Phoebe whined. "Not to me, it isn't."

Europa stopped coughing again. "I'm alright," she lied through her teeth. "Pull me up. I am sick to death of laying down all the time." Phoebe sat up on her knees and pulled her mother into a sitting position. As the blankets fell away, they revealed Europa was wearing a satin peach-colored nightgown and matching sheer drape.

"You sure you're alright?" the young girl dubiously questioned.

"Have you seen Jonathan lately?" her mother answered her question with another question.

"Not much," Phoebe replied. "He came back from Madagascar and then just ran off on another photography job. Something's off; he hasn't been the same since he came back."

"Have you seen your father's hair?" Europa said more than asked. "It's turning grey. He won't tell me what happened down there. I have a feeling it's for the best. I'd take it away if I could." Phoebe just stared at her mother as if she expected something profound to come out next. "I'm feeling a little better today," she spoke again with a groan. "Which isn't saying much," she grinned.

Phoebe just looked at her beaming mother, wondering just how she could smile now.

"Phoebe..." the sick mother started. "You got a bun in the oven, don't you?"

"Be-eh-uh," Phoebe sputtered, taken aback by her mother's brashness. She smirked, then nodded. "How did you know?"

"We can all tell," Europa answered. "Something to do with those traveling pants, I think. I could tell by your complexion."

"Are you... upset?"

"Hell no! I'm very happy about this," Europa replied. "I've been telling your dad how much I wanted a grandkid for years now. He kept telling me to stop wishing our daughter was a slut." They both cackled. "Richard doesn't think any kids should be born right now. Something about two-headed mutations or something... His horror stories kinda run together after a while. If I didn't know him, some of that I could swear he made up."

Phoebe cocked her head with agreement. "I get it," she spoke up. "Look at this trash heap of a world the kid'll grow up in. Even when I was young, things were pretty bad. It's all getting worse."

"You can't worry about that right now," Europa advised. "You will have the baby, won't you? Have you told Jonathan yet?"

"He hasn't been around to tell," Phoebe admitted.

"Be sure to soon," her mother warmly suggested. "He deserves to know." She began coughing again briefly, making Phoebe move back up at attention. "I called my brother," Europa continued to talk. "He said it'd be alright for you to have the baby there in South Imperial Beach where he lives. You should probably go for a visit soon and see how it is. The sea and the air are all clear there. Not quite sure how with all the tequila he pours into himself... That's neither here nor there," she corrected herself. "You wouldn't have to worry about food at all. It's nice and peaceful there he tells me."

"But what about you, mom?" Phoebe half-heartedly protested. "I mean, the whole point of bringing you over here was so someone could take care of you. And now you want me ta go away? Where's the sense there?"

"Your baby is more important," Europa responded.

"Not to me!"

"Your father will be able to care for me just fine."

"Okay, mother..." Phoebe unsurely acquiesced.

"Brock's wife will take good care of the both of you," Europa explained. "She's got a good head on her shoulders. Why she ever married my brother, I'm sure I will never know."

"Cock-drunk, I bet," Phoebe postulated.

"Phoebe!" Europa spat back. "I didn't teach you ta talk like that!"

"Bullshit," her daughter retorted. "You got a mouth on you when you're angry."

The sickly woman did not feel well enough to continue to argue. "Well..." she began again. "You might be scared right now, but I know you're gonna have a lovely child." Her daughter just looked at her. "It's your job now to bring this child into the world, but it will take a lot of hard work. As a mother, it's your duty to take care of it as best you can, regardless of how bad things get. Do you understand?"

"I do, mom..." Phoebe muttered.

Europa sighed as she lay back down onto the couch. "I've already seen in my dreams that my next life will be through your child..."

"Wait, what?!" Phoebe said more than asked.

"I'm feeling a little tired again, sweetie," Europa dismissed her. "Please let me sleep." She began to cough again but only for a moment.

"Do feel better, please," Phoebe almost begged.

"I'll try," Europa whispered as she closed her eyes and smiled.

Phoebe stood up and exited the room, barely able to hold in a crying jag.

A crowd of reporters had congregated around Richard Whisenhunt in his office at the APFE Medical Center. The doctor sat behind his desk as he spoke. He looked visibly aged since his African trip—greying hair, scruffy five o'clock shadow. Madagascar and a dying wife was not agreeing with him at all.

"The disasters are bad, but nothing is more destructive than the misinformation," the doctor informed. "Congress is virtually useless. We'll have to work together as human beings person-to-person if we are to survive. Are you aware that the river in Jordan where Jesus Christ was baptized is so polluted pilgrims can no longer go there? Am I the only one that finds this degree appalling?"

"Dr. Whisenhunt," a young male reporter questioned. "Can you give us any insight into the rise in cancer lately?"

"It's a two-fold problem," Whisenhunt answered. "Holes in the ozone made more dangerous sunlight get through to the Earth. Types of sunlight that our skin usually isn't equipped to handle. We couldn't foresee that jet blowing up, but there was absolutely no reason for the North Koreans to be lobbing nukes around. Particularly in the arctic where the Ozone Layer is especially thin." The desk phone interrupted with a ring. "Excuse me a moment."

The reporters murmured to themselves as Whisenhunt picked up the phone and answered.

"Did he just stop a press conference to answer the phone?" one of the reporters asked his colleagues.

"Hello," Whisenhunt said. "Who's speaking? Oh, it's you... I understand... Yes, I'll try to get back.... It'll be difficult, and I don't know when I'll arrive, but I'll be there. You want to know about what?"

On the other end of the line was Phoebe in the bathroom of her apartment listening to her father on her cell phone. The wiped-away tears just compounded the sadness on her face.

"It may be caused by the Benzoate in the air," Whisenhunt explained. "We're not 100% sure, but it's certainly fatal. Thousands of people just like her are suffering from it. I want you to stay with her until I can get back, okay?"

"Thousands of people aren't my mom..." Phoebe tried to push back but just didn't have any gas left in her tank. "Okay, thanks. Bye."

"Bye, kid."

Phoebe hung up her cell, then buried her face in her hands. The phone dropped to the linoleum-covered floor.

Back in Whisenhunt's office, he'd wasted no time in continuing his media blitz. "The eyes of the world are upon us to see how we will react," he stated. "Unfortunately, our Congress has been bought off by interests that have *no* interest in saving the world. Science told us all this would happen for 80 years. Eighty. Years. The only group that has been dead wrong almost every time are the ones that said science is bullshit. Smoking. Virus. Climate change. Red meat. Pollution... by this point, we've earned extinction. But even without our useless government, we can still show them what we as a people are really made of. We must calm down and face facts. We cannot let this desperate situation get the best of us. We have to think before we do anything foolish."

Madame President Erica Cady paced restlessly in the halls of the White House in D.C. and when she came to a hanging portrait of First Lady Hillary Clinton, she stopped and stared at it. The official portrait did not resemble its subject very much at all. Cady sighed as her thoughts got the better of her.

A few moments later, an official walked up behind her. "Madame President?" he called out to get her attention.

"You know, it shouldn't have been me," Cady spoke up.

"Come again, ma'am?"

"She shoulda been the first woman president," Cady explained, jerking her head toward the portrait of Hillary. "Or at least Kamala. They were way more qualified than I'll ever be."

The official cleared his throat. "I think we've seen well enough that this office doesn't particularly care about qualifications."

"Yeah, but it sure does help," Cady countered in a forlorn tone. "Whaddaya got?"

"Rationing supplies for basic foodstuffs are ready to go into effect," her official explained. "The question now is just when."

"Immediately!" Cady balked as she whirled around.

"Whaddaya mean 'now'?"

"Did I studder, young man?" the president turned on some sass. "As soon as possible. We'll never inspire trust within our people if we don't act and act swiftly." Erica sputtered about unsure of what to say or even do. "I-I need a smoke. And prob'ly a drink."

Back at Phoebe's apartment on the other side of the country, she had left to get some things from Europa's home. Europa had been left alone, sleeping in the living room. Suddenly, the house phone began to ring. Its blaring noise quickly dragged Europa back out of sleep. She looked around, remembering she was all alone right now. Slowly, she began to stir and uneasily pushed herself up and to her feet.

Still draped in blankets, Europa made her way over to the house phone, which was still ringing. Before she picked up, she squinted her eyes to take note of the number on the caller I.D. She didn't recognize the number, but answered anyway. "Hello?" she said in a soft, warm voice.

"You're gonna die, you bitch!" a shrill voice suddenly came over the other end. "You're gonna die slow!" However, it didn't have the apparent desired effect as, in a moment of crystal-clear lucidity, Europa recognized the voice on the other end and took to writing the phone number she'd just seen down on a scrap of paper nearby. It was that incel-nazi she'd beat to hell and back outside the antique store.

"I'm gonna laugh as they lower you—"

"Now look here, you Nazi prick..." Europa interrupted, standing up straighter as she spoke. "I've got your number here. Soon, I'll have your address and after that... *I'll be there.* And when I leave... I'll be taking your punk-ass, limp-dick Nazi scalp with me, motherfu—" The phone hung up on the other end. Europa suddenly began to breathe shallowly as if all her energy had been put into verbally bitchslapping that delinquent.

"S'what I thought..." she gasped as she leaned her head against the wall then closed her eyes and began to cough again.

CHAPTER 10 - Death of a Loving Thing

The traffic of the 405 highway in Los Angeles was backed up bumper to bumper... nearly five times worse than usual. Nobody seemed to be advancing at all. Horns honked and people grew impatient. Some drivers stuck their heads out the windows in search of sneaky ways out. Others were completely out on the road, distraught at the situation before them. One especially impatient annoyed driver was the incel-nazi. Apparently, Europa's threats had scared him enough to flee. Or attempt it anyway.

Jonathan was there, moving amongst the cars, snapping photos of the gridlock from hell.

Babies cried, exhausts smoked, and engines revved. So much so that a new cloud of exhaust was beginning to hang over the immediate area.

By nighttime, things had become no better. In fact, the cars probably hadn't even moved an inch. The noise was louder and people were now yelling and very angry. A couple in one car proceeded to make out in the front seat to pass the time.

The incel-nazi couldn't take this madness anymore and had had enough. "Aw, fuck this," he hissed before throwing his car into gear. The vehicle uneasily began making its way between cars, knocking some of them out of the way like a game of bumper cars. Before too long, however, the car hit between two other cars spaced closely together and shot into the air. A driver with his family watched the car as it sailed overhead.

The incel-nazi's car came down, colliding with the gas tank of another car, causing it to explode. The one ahead of that caused the next car to explode and so on like a fiery game of dominoes. It did not take long before the 405 was covered with nothing but flames. Some people tried to get away. One woman was crushed by the hull of a charred car. Others exited their own cars, already burning themselves.

Flaming cars and wreckage littered the highway. Smoke and flame soon obscured the immediate area. The flames reached high into the air as if a city of fire had suddenly appeared.

In Phoebe's apartment, Phoebe and Europa were huddled together on the couch with the remnants of Chinese food splayed out around them. The two watched reports of the disaster on television. Europa shook her head fearfully while Phoebe clutched at her mother's hand.

Elsewhere in Los Angeles, teenagers partied with reckless abandon. Some smoked crack, others shot up or tied off. Others partook in various sexual acts because why the hell not? Their future was gone anyway. Some had banners up that read, "*Embrace the End.*"

A small five-year-old stood alone amongst the middle of this, watching with confusion.

In another place, two teenage boys grabbed a teenage girl and ran off with her, carrying her off the ground by her upper arms, and completely ignoring her panicked protests.

Other teens lined up against building walls loitering like there was no tomorrow. They looked very much like the living dead in the Madagascar cave... but doing so of their own volition.

"The world will end when the twelfth monkey evolves into a human being," one of the boys muttered out of nowhere to no one in particular.

Somewhere else, two cis male white-trash bullies beat on a defenseless trans woman pinned against the ground. Their assault was savage, the seeming aim to kill her.

In Whitehorse, Canada, the city's animal control team did their best to fend off a trio of polar bears, who had invaded the Yukon territory town in search of food. There were already some human corpses about nearby, all of them appearing as if they'd been chewed on.

One polar bear lunged forward and got a man by the throat. The tranquilizer darts subsequently fired upon it had no results. Instead, the bear chomped down its powerful jaws, beheading the poor victim in its mouth.

It did not look good for the humans.

Outside a government warehouse, an angry, noisy crowd of people clamored for food rations. Armed guards tried their best to keep the crowd from doing much more than rabble rouse. A metal sheet door opened and more guards packing firepower appeared to keep the crowd in check.

"People, please calm down!" the lead guard called out for attention. "Everyone is ordered to leave here, right now!"

"You can't give us orders!" a young man shouted.

"That's literally my job here, kid," the guard volleyed back.

Some people in the crowd began fighting with the guards, throwing punches. The guards had not yet gotten violent other than trying to keep the crowd back with their rifles and other manners of force.

"If you do not leave the premises immediately," the lead guard called out. "You will force us to place all of you under arrest!"

Arrest or not, the guards began to beat some of the people in the crowd, either with their fists, rifles, or nightsticks. Eventually, people got the message and slowly dispersed. The guards themselves tried to relax as things got under control once more.

On a highway leading into Los Angeles, there was sparse traffic on either side. An old mini-camper sputtered its way down the road. Inside, Phoebe and her uncle Brock sat across from one another listening to news on the radio. Phoebe looked uneasy. Behind them was a gun rack, complete with rifles at the ready, on the rear window.

Brock was a tall, muscular fellow with blue eyes and dirty blonde hair that looked something like a Caesar hairstyle. He was dressed in a white t-shirt with red collar and jeans.

"The polar bears are becoming more and more hostile," the radio announcer informed, "and aren't afraid to go after human beings. No reports yet of any such occurrences in the lower forty-eight, but scientists expect it to be only a matter of time. Similarly, people have begun to riot in the streets, trying to get at the government's food rationing programs. So far, nothing violent has occurred, but police officials are prepared for the worst."

Brock switched the radio off, groaning with disgust. "Lazy asses," he hissed in a low-toned voice. "If they want more food, they can go hunt it, just like the rest of us."

"Brock, do you really think we should be doing this?" Phoebe uneasily queried.

"Doin' what, sweetheart?" the driver answered her question with a question.

"It sounds like grave robbing to me..." his passenger continued. "It's creepy."

"Maybe," Brock admitted. "But they're not gonna need their things anymore. Besides, don't you want to see your mom?"

"Well yeah," Phoebe replied. "But does robbing the dead really need to be an excuse to see her?"

"Look," the blond man began. "What if we go there and find like a distressed puppy or something? Couldn't you use a puppy for that baby to play with?"

"I suppose..." Phoebe grumbled.

"And isn't that a lot better than that dog dying of hunger or neglect?" Brock pressed. "Tell you what, Phoebes. We'll go see your mom first."

Later that day, Brock and Phoebe had made it to the area of the 405 where the car disasters had occurred. The entire highway was littered with the burnt-out husks of vehicles. The whole area had just been shut down and made inaccessible by cars because there was just too much wreckage to deal with. Fortunately, the corpses had been attended to and taken away.

Brock moved from car to car, trying to find something of value to steal. Occasionally, he came across some kind of trinket and pocketed it. Phoebe stood against the median partition with her arms across her chest, looking appropriately disturbed and disapproving.

"Mom looked really bad," Phoebe reflected on her visit.

"I know," her uncle agreed. "Poor thing. Rough seeing her like that. She wasn't that pale before was she?"

"No," Phoebe answered. "I wish Jonathan would come for a visit..."

"Isn't he busy workin' with your dad?" Brock groaned as he jimmied a locked door.

"Yeah," the young lady sighed. "But he could at least call. I haven't got to tell him about the, well... you know."

Brock pulled his head out of a car hull too quickly, banging his head on its window frame with a shout. "You haven't told him?!" he incredulously asked as he rubbed the back of his head.

"No," Phoebe said. "And I haven't told my dad either."

"Well, ya gotta!" Brock proclaimed, "Next time you talk to him, you have to tell him."

"Yeah..." Phoebe begrudgingly agreed as she turned and began to wander around. "That's what mom told me too."

"That's cause your mom's a smart gal," Brock stated as he went back to raiding the wrecks.

"I used to think more positively," Phoebe mused as she walked. "I used to think people could solve anything we put our minds to."

"Shit!" Brock screeched after opening up an empty glove compartment, not listening.

"But looking at everything that's going on right now, I don't know," the young woman continued. "I don't know if people even want to make things better. Everyone just seems to want to accept it and ride out the end."

"Jackpot!" Brock announced.

Phoebe turned her attention back to her uncle's unusual proclivity. "What is it?" she inquired.

"I found a hunner'd dollar bill with minimum char damage," Brock reported.

"I want half," Phoebe shot back.

Meanwhile, in the inner streets of L.A., the rioters had regrouped... under a dangerous new leader. The crowd had grown to immense proportions and sported rudimentary weapons like knives and batons.

Their leader was a snow-white man in his late 30s with a shaved head. He wore a dark overcoat with a red band around the left arm.

"We'll never get the food we want unless we take it!" the new Nazi leader shouted, resulting in cheers from the crowd. "Aren't you tired of being hungry all the time? This isn't the America I grew up in... where they told you how much and what you can eat! I'd rather be dead than not allowed to have a steak!" The crowd again cheered in agreement. "Life can't go on like this. Action is what we need and now!"

The nearby crowd cheered its approval. Jonathan weaved in and out among them, snapping off photographs whenever possible.

"The food that we need is in those government warehouses!" the head Nazi asserted. "I say it's time we take 'em! There's enough for everybody in there! If they will not give, we will take!"

The surrounding crowd let loose with a roar of cheers. Their Nazi leader charged with his followers in tow. Jonathan was immediately swamped by the running people.

The crowd picked up others as it moved along in the middle of Los Angeles city streets in broad daylight. The crowd itself grew larger, angrier, and louder. It all looked like very bad news.

At Phoebe's apartment, Richard Whisenhunt was there with Europa on the couch watching a news report covering the riot. Her hair had completely went back to its original black color. She cuddled in against him as he hooked his left arm around her. However, they were both horrified by what was unfolding before them.

"God. Damn Nazis," the sick woman hissed.

"They ruin everything," her husband sighed. "I thought we settled this shit over 100 years ago?"

Europa shook her head with disapproval.

At a meeting in the Situation Room in the White House in Washington D.C., Madame President Cady and some of her officials sat around an intimate table.

"It's not just in Los Angeles," Chiang explained. "There are food riots everywhere. Even in other countries like Russia, England, and Japan. Unless we do something soon, anarchy could spread throughout the country."

"We have to keep a watch on these radical splinter groups too," Jergens suggested. "They may choose now as a time to start a revolution. We should act now before it's too late."

"Madame President..." Chiang pleaded. "Give us an order to immediately mobilize the national guard."

Cady sighed with dissatisfaction. "Nope," she blurted out. "I will not do that."

"And why on earth not?!" Jergens demanded to know. "Our laws must be enforced... especially now!"

"These are not riots," the president explained. "Nor are they necessarily unlawful."

"Is that so?" Senator Selzner balked. "Then what would you call them?"

"People's stomachs tell them to go where food is," Cady explained. "Whether that be McDonald's or Burger King or our stockpile warehouses. When they're stopped, there's going to be trouble. So, just let 'em go."

"There's already enough trouble," Senator Avalon chimed in. "The food rationing will be enough. No one will starve and they can keep all of their jobs. Just let us deploy the national guard to stifle these uprisings."

"Richard Whisenhunt once said something that I'll never forget," Madame President began. "In order for government to work properly, it has to have the trust of the people. We have lost that, gentlemen. And there's probably no way we can get it back." President Cady pushed her chair back, then rose to her feet. "I told you all that it would be very difficult to overcome this crisis without their trust," she continued. "It's our own fault our credibility is shot to hell. But what we need right now is a little patience. We've got to wait until this mass panic is over and common sense returns to people once more."

Meanwhile in Los Angeles, the riots were, in fact, riots. The gaggle of Nazis smashed their way into a Jack in the Box, taking down windows and doors in their path. Their dear leader stood outside and issued commands as others did the actual breaking and entering. They used whatever tools they had on hand to smash through the glass windows.

Later, there were rioters on the roof of the building, throwing down boxes of food to those below. Some ran off with their ill-gotten meals. Others just opened the boxes right then and there. The Leader shouted instructions to the others.

Elsewhere, the Nazi-lead rioters used their tools to open up the metal sheet doors at the government warehouse from which they had previously been driven away. It did not take them long to have busted their way inside.

Once in, the rioters grabbed everything they could get their selfish mitts on: food, water, snack foods. The entire warehouse was filled to the brim with rioters snatching everything in sight. A pile of oranges was grabbed clear within seconds.

Jonathan had foolishly been following the rioter's exploits and was there snapping photos. His activity got the attention of the mob's leader.

"Get outta here, narc!" the bald Nazi shouted before punching him in the left eye.

Others grabbed bottles of champagne, popped them open, and downed them on the spot.

At a second government warehouse, the metal sheet doors flew open and the army of rioters charged in. Inside were bags of grain which soon fell prey to the horde. They descended on the bags like flies, tossing them down to other rioters below. Once they were suitably placated, the crowd marched out again with their bags of raw food in tow, cheering triumphantly.

Despite the president's reservations, most of what these people were doing was by-god illegal. Fires burnt in trash cans. Front windows of stores were busted out and looting was rampant. Whatever the rioters could get their hands on were carried off. Their Nazi leader stood upon an overturned car, pointing a stick and shouting commands to his followers like an unholy Moses.

Whole city blocks were on fire. The firefighters did their best to smother the raging inferno with sprays of water.

"The riots in Los Angeles have taken a turn for the worse," Silliman the news anchor explained. "Fires rage and power is out all over the city. Citizens are urged to stay indoors and if possible, arm yourself for protective purposes only."

Armed guards just looked at one another and shrugged before putting away their nightsticks and replacing their rifles over their backs. They just gave in to a literal mob rule.

Back at Phoebe and Jonathan's place, Europa had retired to the bedroom where she lay in bed and was a deathly pale white color. A variety of flowers from well-meaning well-wishers decorated the room. Whisenhunt was sitting up in bed next to her.

"Please don't hate me for this," Europa spoke haltingly through labored breathing.

"For what?" Whisenhunt asked for clarification.

"For leaving you like this," Europa answered. "At a time like this. Please don't hate me, darling."

"My love for you is just a strong as it was the day we married," the doctor avowed.

Europa smiled. "Have you heard the good news yet, Richard?" she questioned.

"What news is that, sweetie?" her husband replied. "I could use some good news."

"Phoebe—" Europa began but was interrupted by a cough. "Phoebe's going to have a child."

"No, I hadn't heard," the doctor replied. "I haven't seen Phoebe for a while. How long has she been pregnant? Do you know?"

"Oh, three months or so, I think," Europa surmised. "Not long. She certainly isn't showing. I want her to have it, Richard."

Whisenhunt looked off, rather unsure of how to respond.

"I know how you feel about things, dear," Europa uncertainly began again. "And that horrible thing that happened to Sam and his daughter... But just you wait—wait until you see it. It's going to be a beautiful child. You're going to love it, I just know you will."

Whisenhunt smiled at his wife's optimism. "Europa always tells the truth," he stated. "Do you know where Phoebe is now?"

"I sent her to my brother's to stay down near Mexico," the ailing wife answered. "She's going to have the baby there. Someplace she can relax and not worry about the rest of the world."

"That's a very good idea," her husband admitted.

Europa breathed heavily. "I know I'm about to go," she spoke through her breaths. "But someday I'm going to return. I think the Earth is like that too. I think the Earth is going to die and be reborn once again. When the Earth is born again and we both come back, I'll be your wife again and we can do this life thing right."

"I think we did alright this time," Whisenhunt said. "It's the world that failed us."

"Do you not like that idea?" his wife inquired.

"I found you in this life," Whisenhunt replied. "I can find you in the next. Here's to someday." He pulled up Europa's hand and kissed her fingers. "But right now, I think you need to get some rest."

"No," Europa forcefully responded. "If I go to sleep... I'm not waking up again..." She began to slowly stir and groaned and she pushed herself to sit up next to her husband. After she had managed to do so, she turned to face him, but her breathing sharpened. "It's not fair, Richard," she decreed.

"What isn't?"

"Our anniversary's coming up soon... I didn't want to spend it dead."

Europa raised her hand, still clutching around her husband's fingers. "Can you feel my hand?" she asked.

"Of course I do, darling."

"I can't..."

That statement hit Whisenhunt like a ton of bricks as he realized the implications. Europa leaned against him, still holding his hand. She draped her head over his shoulder as her hair cascaded around her face.

"It's a wonderful feeling," Europa began in a soft, weak voice. "There's a voice, Richard... My mother is calling my name."

Tears uncontrollably began streaming from Whisenhunt's eyes but he did his best to hold it together for his wife.

"There are beautiful flowers here..." Europa barely continued. "The colors are like paintings. It's a lovely new world... The people there are calling out to me."

"Europa?" Whisenhunt said more than asked in a panic. "Europa?"

"I'm so tired, darling," his wife hissed like air was leaving her body. "I'm going back to sleep."

"Europa?" Whisenhunt gently smacked the side of her face. "Please don't sleep Europa."

The dying woman wearily pulled herself back to face her husband. "I—I—" she choked out.

"Europa?"

"I love you, Richard..."

"I love you too, Europa."

"...Always..."

"Europa?" Whisenhunt panicked anew. There was no response. "Europa? Can you hear me? Europa?"

Europa's eyes slowly closed and her lips quivered. "Hope..." softly passed through them.

"What, Europa?" her husband hurriedly said.

"They say... Hope for future..." With a last gasp, Europa died. Despite knowing better, Whisenhunt futilely tried to awaken her but Europa was gone. Giving up, he laid her body back onto the bed and lay his head on her still chest, weeping uncontrollably.

Memories of himself and his wife in their glory days flooded the bereaved man's mind. In no short order, he saw—

—a younger Whisenhunt walking underneath a tree in a lovely gentle field. Something grabbed his attention as he passed and he turned and looked upward to find a younger, giggling black-haired Europa sitting on a tree limb. She laughed. "You found me."

—Whisenhunt lifted Europa's veil at their wedding and they kissed.

—And they kissed.

—And they kissed.

—And they kissed.

—The two were in a hospital bed, fawning over the birth of their new daughter.

—Europa sat in a rocking chair cradling baby Phoebe.

—A now blonde-haired Europa entered a room with a smile and a tray with a bowl of soup.

—Europa lay across from Whisenhunt in their bed, smiling.

— Whisenhunt and Europa threw their hands up and shouted general disgruntlements as they saw the re-rise of Nazism on television being permitted like it was nothing.

—In the dead of one Christmas Eve night, as both were dressed in black, Europa, wearing a black sock cap, kept watch with a flashlight while behind her, Whisenhunt relieved himself on the grave of Donald Trump at Mar-a-Largo. After he was done, the two high-fived, Europa turned out her flashlight, and they fled like thieves in the night.

Back in the apartment, the doctor picked up Europa's corpse and cradled her in his arms. Shortly thereafter, the sound of pounding footsteps could be heard approaching. Jonathan turned a corner and entered the bedroom, a bruise on his face where he'd been hit. As he saw what had happened, his jaw dropped to the floor and he froze with shock.

Whisenhunt slowly looked up at him, a pathetic and broken figure. "She's dead..." he just barely got out.

Jonathan involuntarily dropped to the floor and after a few moments, began to cry.

"Jonathan..." Whisenhunt whispered. "Jonathan!" he repeated more forcefully. The young man looked up at him and sniffled. "Go upstairs to the roof, please. I'll be with you in a minute."

Jonathan nodded his head a few times, then got up and started to walk out of the room. He then stopped himself and turned back around. "Uh... I may not have a key to the roof," he explained.

"Then kick the fucking door down and blame it on rioters," Whisenhunt shot back. "I need some fresh air."

Jonathan went to leave again. Whisenhunt turned his head to listen for the door to close. When he heard it a few moments later, he gently lowered Europa's corpse back onto the ground. Then, he wearily pushed himself back to his feet.

The doctor looked down at the floor and at the body of his wife as if in deep contemplation. And then, out of nowhere—

"HOW COULD YOU LET THIS HAP-PEN??!" Whisenhunt angrily shouted. "What kind of God lets this happen?! You see this, don't you?! Not just this, but... *this* !" he gestured to everything around him. "Europa *didn't* deserve this! *Patrice didn't deserve this*! How is destroying them part of your fucking plan?! How is that just? How is that caring? WHY ARE YOU LETTING THIS HAPPEN TO YOUR WORLD?!?"

No answers were forthcoming. Whisenhunt slumped to the floor on his knees where he looked over at Europa's corpse once again. The resultant silence was deafening.

Up on the roof of the apartment building, Jonathan was in luck, because the door to the roof was unlocked and he was just able to pass through. Currently though, while smoke occasionally could be spotted lifting upward, the air was generally calmer-looking than when the riots were fully on. Whisenhunt and Jonathan stood side by side at the edge of the rooftop as the sound of emergency vehicle sirens could be heard in the distance. Whisenhunt looked like someone had just shaken the life out of him.

"The quiet makes me think all that down there in the city is just a bad dream," Jonathan spoke up.

"I don't think there's an end to this nightmare," Whisenhunt flatly said. "It'll likely get a lot worse. Worse-er."

"You really think that the end is near?"

"Yes, it is," the doctor admitted. "I can feel it creeping up like a baaaad case of hives. But there are some things we haven't tried yet that might help. Jonathan... will you go to Phoebe down near Mexico-way and tell her that Europa has died?"

"I will."

"And if possible, I'd like you to stay with her," Whisenhunt continued. "With things like this, God knows what'll happen. And put a ring on that girl's finger, dummy. I'll give you one of Europa's to take. She doesn't need them anymore."

Jonathan turned and outstretched his right arm to Whisenhunt for a handshake. The doctor saw it and moved to shake but then pulled the young man in for a hug.

"But what about you?" Jonathan asked as he pulled away.

"I'll just stay right here and wait for Dooms-day," Whisenhunt answered. "Maybe go Bronson on somma those Nazis down there while I wait. Ask 'em if they believe in Jesus. Let 'em know they're gonna meet him. It's what Europa would've wanted."

Jonathan looked over at Whisenhunt, legitimately taken aback. "That might be a little on the danger-ous side," he finally said.

"Like I've got anything to lose..." the doctor half-answered with a huff.

Just then, something in the sky grabbed Jonathan's attention. The ambiance suddenly became dingy and green. "Doctor?" he called out to see if someone else was seeing it too. Whisenhunt looked out across the skyline with an 'it figures' look on his face.

"Richard?!" Jonathan called out again. Whisenhunt raised his right hand and gave a flourishing gesture as if to present something but his facial expression was little more than dull surprise.

The sky above the horizon of buildings was an exact upside-down reflection of the city below it. Like a city in the sky. The rioters in the streets stopped and took notice as well. They dropped their ill-gotten gains and began a mass panic.

"It's the end of the world!" a man shouted.

"The end of the world!" another parroted.

Even their Nazi leader couldn't believe what he was seeing. Was it a sign of the end from God? A reckoning for their criminal activities?

"The smog is beginning to affect our atmosphere," Whisenhunt explained, gesturing to the sky above. "The clouds in the sky are acting like a giant mirror now, reflecting the landscape down here upside down."

Jonathan snapped off a series of frenzied photographs.

CHAPTER 11 - Vida Eterna

Foamy waves from the Pacific rolled onto the shoreline at the South Imperial Beach. Jonathan sat in some safe dry sand whilst Phoebe stood stock still in the tide as water rushed in all around her legs. She was wearing a white blouse with sheer sleeves, matching white shorts that ended at the upper thigh, and knee-high white boots that gave her the appearance of an angelic showgirl.

Having been informed of her mother's demise, Phoebe had spent about a half hour sobbing. By now, she had managed to dry up but for the last ten minutes, she had engaged in a thousand-yard-stare with the ocean's horizon. The sound of the water flowing in and out had brought her some semblance of calm.

"Hey, isn't this the beach where Rocky outran Apollo Creed?" Jonathan questioned as he looked around. Phoebe ignored his query with extreme prejudice. She had stopped crying, but her face was stained with the tracks of her tears. Her disassociation was becoming troubling to Jonathan. He began to worry that his news had broken her mind and in a way, it had.

"No," Phoebe finally spoke. Jonathan perked up because it seemed to him like a statue just began talking to him. "But there are some good fish tacos at the end of the pier."

Having returned to her proper state of consciousness, Phoebe bent down and used the incoming sea water to wash her face clean, removing the salt and smeared eyeliner from her cheeks. Finally, she turned to face Jonathan, who was occupied harassing a poor crab that was just trying to get back to the sea.

"Hey Jonathan, stop playing with that crab and pay some attention," she chided. "We're having a baby."

"What?" Jonathan legitimately questioned as he let the crab go on its way. The crustacean clamped its pincers together as it crawled away sideways. "I didn't understand you. What'd you say?"

"A baby, Jon," Phoebe repeated with emphasis. "'Baby'. I'm having one." The news struck Jonathan like a head-on collision. He didn't actually say "Holy shit," but he was thinking it *very* loudly. "One life has left the Earth..." she continued. "And another has come to replace it. My mother believed that her next life would be through my child... and she wanted me to have it."

"Will you?" her boyfriend pressed.

"Of course, I will. Someone left my cake out in the rain. I don't think that I can take it, cause it took so long to bake it. And we'll never have this recipe agaaain. Oh, noooooo..." Phoebe made over-the-top dramatic postures and gestures as she sang.

Jonathan jumped to his feet to join his girl-friend's position. "Phoebes, you worry me."

"I recall the yellow cotton dress foaming like a wave on the ground around your knees," Phoebe sang-spoke as she weaved this way and that around Jonathan like she was about to dribble past him in a basketball game to troll him.

"You know your father wouldn't agree," Jonathan spoke up to try to get her mind right again.

Phoebe's mischievous grin faded away into a more serious countenance. "It's not his baby," she spoke up. "It's our baby. *My* baby.... baby."

"That it's not."

"It is my duty to raise this child as best I can, regardless of how rough things are," Phoebe said.

"But now?" Jonathan questioned. "I have to be here and I don't want to be here anymore. I can't even imagine what that kid'll have to go through."

"They won't be going through it alone," Phoebe shot back. "Just like we're not. I'm the one who let myself get pregnant, so the responsibility lies with me. Probably more us, but certainly me. The thought of anything going wrong with this child scares me."

"In that case then, why not reconsider?" her boyfriend said more than asked.

"If we take this gamble and it pays off," Phoebe explained, "then that furthers the cause of the human race. If we killed it, we would be turning our back on the human race's future."

"Eh—what?" Jonathan muttered in confusion.

"Aren't you happy to be a father?" Phoebe switched lanes.

"Well... sure I am, sweetie..." Jonathan stumbled through an answer. He was not selling it.

"Stop your worrying!" Phoebe ordered. "Nothing's going to happen to this child. We won't let it. I have to have it for my mother. How will she come back if I destroy her vessel?" She slowly backed away from Jonathan, striking a pose to display herself to him. "This is a new life growing inside me. Our baby, Jonathan. Our baby will save the world."

In sync, Jonathan and Phoebe closed the gap between themselves and sealed it with a kiss.

"See?" Phoebe said more than asked. "Getting better." Behind Jonathan, she could see a set of sandy rolling hills in the distance. She gently used her hand to push his chin to turn his face and see them as well. "Race ya to the top."

"I'm in no shape to be runnin' that far," Jonathan replied.

"Whatsamatter? Afraid a pregnant girl'll beat your ass?" Phoebe said with maximum snark, all but punctuating it with a "bawk-bawk-bawk."

"Oh, you're gonna eat my dust, baby," Jonathan man'd up.

Phoebe suddenly pushed her boyfriend onto the sand and charged off, creating a cheap advantage. "What???" was all Jonathan could manage to sputter.

"Viva Europa Whisenhunt!" Phoebe proclaimed to the universe as Jonathan clambered back to his feet way behind her and gave chase. The two ran at full sprint speed along the length of the beach, but Jonathan was just too far behind and too sluggish to catch Phoebe.

"Phoebe, where are you going?!" the young man breathlessly demanded to know.

"To dance!"

"But your doctor said— !" Jonathan impotently protested.

"Screw 'im!" Phoebe barked with authority.

As the sun went down in the far Pacific distance, its light cast everything in sight in hues of Frost-
esque gold, Phoebe ran over the top of the sandy hill
then came to a stop as choreography began to form in
her mind. Jonathan limped behind just in time to see
Phoebe begin to dance. And dance. And dance. Like
there was literally no tomorrow.

She was dancing. Really dancing. Arms and legs
flailing around her, she whirled around and jumped
her happiness into the seaside air. Foot forward. Back.
Left arm up. Like an improvisational game of Twister.
Phoebe couldn't remember the last time she'd done
this—or why she had ever stopped. Cause some man
told her she couldn't? The flashing golden colors of
the sky in her blurry vision momentarily blinded but
did not deter her.

Phoebe slowed down her momentum and
stopped. The lowering sunlight turned her into a
silhouette of delight. Her hips swayed, her waist
swiveled, and her hair fluttered about in the breeze as
her arms waved around above her head when she
suddenly pulled her right leg up against her body, then
began to spin around in circles, balanced by her arms
but bolstered only by her lone, seemingly-healed left
leg.

The pollution in the air which had earlier that
day created a terrifying apocalyptic image was now
causing a vision of concentrated beauty: the refracted
light of the polluted sky now made it look as if there
were *four* suns setting at once.

Jonathan's eyes cut toward the sky and he was
taken aback as he saw what was in the air above his

baby mama. As the rings of orange light halo'd over Phoebe, Jonathan questioned to himself if this was a sign from the universe that his girlfriend was secretly some kind of angel or goddess. Was she doing this with her very will? Could their baby really save the world??? And there was Phoebe dancing beneath it all, jumping about like a child trying to reach a top shelf from the floor.

As Phoebe celebrated her mother's life and soul, nothing—not even the end of the world—could erase the joy in her heart.

CHAPTER 12 - Catastrophe 2050

Flags whipped about in the breeze around the U.S. Capitol Building on Capitol Hill in Washington D.C. With the world's disasters on the rise—particularly the bizarre sky occurrence along the west coast—Madame President Cady had summoned Richard Whisenhunt to the nation's capitol to address its lawmakers in a last ditch effort into scaring them into doing *something*.

Inside, Whisenhunt stood where many a'president had stood before on the floor of the United States House of Representatives chamber. He looked more aged and tired than before. Cady sat nearby to the side at attention. Whisenhunt was surrounded by the entirety of the nation's representatives and senators. A handful of them took the risk of censures in order to avoid what would assuredly be "Whisenhunt's bogus woke talk."

Jonathan and Phoebe were on hand as well, dressed in their Sunday best: Jonathan was in a black blazer and matching slacks and Phoebe wore the same dress her mother had worn during the newspaper interview in which she'd participated. Both now wore modest wedding rings on their left hands; Phoebe's still had a sparkly diamond on it.

Lee Silliman was also on hand to cover the event, situated in a plum spot in the audience and scribbling notes in a large notepad.

"All of the most recent events in the world," Whisenhunt addressed the lawmakers, "almost certainly point to a dreadful imminent calamity. At the same time, as the major cities were falling into chaos because of food riots, the other strange occurrences drove many people into a state of fear. Some people even died of fright. Rainwater is no longer safe to drink... *anywhere* on the Earth. It's too poisoned by the atmosphere it has to fall through. Acute anxiety and confusion is widespread."

On Japan's main Honshu island along the Fossa Magna rift, Asama Volcano, one of the many volcanoes along that range, suddenly exploded. It wasn't just an eruption—the cone of the volcano blew up. Dirt and rock flew everywhere. Smoke started drifting into the air. Soon after, magma became lava and spewed forth onto land, coating the immediate grounds nearby.

"What if a calamity did occur and make things worse than they are now?" Whisenhunt postulated. "Volcanoes and earthquake areas could be triggered off easily by some great cataclysm. If that occurred, the results would be horrible. The nation of Japan could be destroyed in a series of eruptions!"

In Los Angeles, a rumbling abruptly began deep within the city. Almost immediately following, a full-scale earthquake began, shaking buildings to the very foundations. People on the street ran, trying to avoid falling rubble. An unfortunate victim's body slumped against a wall. A bruised woman tried to push herself back to her feet but her body wasn't cooperating. Buildings everywhere fell into themselves.

The Heysham Nuclear Power Station on the shore of Great Britain suddenly exploded. In the skies over Liverpool, flashes went off signaling the destruction of the Ozone Layer there. Light shone down brightly upon the shrieking citizens below. The city itself began to burn in seconds. An oil refinery exploded. People grabbed their belongings out of nearby office buildings and ran for cover. An entire Liverpool shoreline went up in explosive flames.

By nightfall out at sea, the waters parted to reveal the presence of a monster whale-like creature likely mutated by runoff in the ocean. Only its head could be seen and that was still partially submerged. It appeared to be that of a sperm whale—boxy with a long, narrow jaw and full of pointy teeth. The eyes rolled about to see what it could see on land. The creature was planning to come ashore somehow and vent its rage on land.

However, the sea-thing had picked the wrong night to begin an assault on the Englishsters because the shoreline was still raging with bright orange fire that lit up the night sky. The whale monster studied this inferno it would have to pass through, but eventually decided it was not worth it and just dove back beneath the waves again. Only it knew where it was headed now.

"England could sink into the ocean," Whisenhunt explained. "The United States could be wracked with earthquakes. And said earthquakes could cause awful nuclear disasters at our plants. Essentially, there's no safeguard when it comes to nuclear power. The consequences of nuclear pollution are truly terrible. And despite an almost worldwide demand, halt to nuclear testing is still far from a reality."

Later at the disaster in Liverpool, destruction and debris were the only things left. Charred corpses littered the ground. Out of nowhere, a heavy rain started up, making the whole thing even messier-looking.

Elsewhere, a military jet flew through the air doing reconnaissance. In an ocean nearby, a submarine plowed through the sea, doing its own form of reconnaissance. An aircraft carrier in the vicinity launched a squadron of jets, who zoomed off into the sky from the carrier's runway.

There was suddenly a battle in a war with Russia, being fought in the barren woodlands of North Korea. Somehow this battle was down to the United States and France vs. the Russians with an assist by North Korea. Radio-controlled M270 MLRS missile launchers and M1A2 SEP Abrams tanks rolled into the battlefield. A French NH90 helicopter hovered overhead to oversee the upcoming conflict.

As the U.S. tanks and missile launchers advanced, Russian TOS-1A Solntsepek MRL missile launchers turned and took aim at their oncoming enemies. Without warning, Russian T-72 tanks opened fire. The M270s continued their procession as the ground around them exploded dirt into the air. They then came to a stop and quickly opened return fire, blasting off their own missiles as the ground around them detonated. The missiles sailed across the wasteland and some managed to hit the TOS-1A MRLs and the T-72s in rapid but powerful explosions.

Some of the M270s rolled on as they fired. A squadron of North Korean MiG-29 jets zoomed in out of the sky like they had used the clouds themselves for cover. They wasted no time in opening fire with mini-nuclear warheads. The missiles found their mark on the M270s, causing them to explode in a larger than usual blast. Shrapnel of the radio-controlled hardware flew everywhere. One of the jets fired another mini-warhead, utterly destroying the French NH90 as well as those on board.

The turrets of the M1A2 SEP tanks slowly took aim and, as soon as they were in position, opened fire. A round managed to hit one of the MiGs, destroying it in mid-air with the resultant shrapnel still flying from inertia alone. Try as they might, the M1A2s and M270s were no match for nuclear weapons and were soon wiped out.

When the battle was over, the barren woodland looked even more desolate as the remnants of military hardware blasted to kingdom come littered the region. On the easternmost side, the corpses of Russian solders had been reduced to piles of human-shaped ashes by the use of nuclear warheads. An oncoming breeze caused their remains to be scattered to the wind.

"The world powers are too egotistical," Whisenhunt commented. "A worldwide war between east and west is not just possible but probable. Even if it's just a local war, there's still the risk. Even if it's just a local war—once the nuclear bomb is used—mankind can just go ahead and call it a life."

The submarine prowling the depths of the sea let loose with a missile. It broke the surface of the ocean and continued sailing higher into the air. It was followed by another missile... and another.

At the Dombarovsky nuclear missile base in the middle of Russian nowhere, a soldier's hand pushed a key into a lock and turned. Almost immediately, an alarm began to blare. Outside the hillside base, a door opened up with a clang, revealing a nuclear missile underneath. The missile suddenly came to life and blasted off into the air. It began to sail into a curved trajectory.

Another missile followed suit. Then another. And...

At the Malmstrom Air Force Base in Montana, nuclear missile after nuclear missile blasted off into the sky. Inside, buttons lit up along with a warning alarm, which read *"Prepare to fire."* Sure enough, the jets of a nuclear missile blasted on and lifted it into the air. The door of the missile silo opened and the nuclear missile zoomed off.

Missile after missile after missile blasted into the air hellbound for their targets.

"If something—anything—catastrophic were to cause a World War III," Whisenhunt warned, "the ensuing nuclear apocalypse would be mankind's death rattle."

Over the skies of London, a flash zoomed out over the entire city and it suddenly detonated, sending debris everywhere, The famous Tower Bridge exploded into a mere pile of twisted wreckage.

A flash shot out over the skies of New York City and it subsequently exploded, sending its own debris everywhere. The Statue of Liberty was beheaded by errant wreckage and the rest of it toppled off its pedestal and fell over into the sea.

A flash blasted out over the Vatican in Rome and it too exploded. People out and about for their daily routine were vaporized in an instant. Some of their shadows were charred into the ground.

A bright light flashed over the Arc de Triumph in Paris when it suddenly shattered into pieces, along with everything around it. Twisted chunks of the Eiffel Tower flew into the Seine River as its body crumbled and fell over.

In the Huairou District in China, a healthy young woman felt pleased with herself as she transversed the Great Wall of China. She'd almost made it from one side to the other. But then, the sky flashed and not only she, but other tourists, and the Great Wall itself were all obliterated in an instant.

A bright light flashed over the people of Madrid. It, too, exploded, annihilating everything and everyone below.

A massive skyscraper just exploded into nothingness.

A crowded baseball stadium was immediately obliterated.

Building after building, city after city, human life after human life was destroyed in the nuclear holocaust. It was if the entire Earth was exploding everywhere at once.

At Buchel Air Base in Germany, the missiles were still launching, even *with* incoming nuclear missiles appearing nearby. They exploded while still high in the sky. The blinding flash of light and resultant explosion was four times more powerful than normal.

Incoming missiles were spotted as outgoing missiles blasted off at the Kozelsk base in Russia. There was another flash and another nuclear explosion. Base after base after base—from Warren Air Force Base in Wyoming to the Bhabha Atomic Research Center in India to the Royal Naval Armament Depot in Great Britain—was destroyed by incoming nuclear missiles from what used to be Earth's countries. The sky just turned into a flash of blinding bright light and hazy smoke.

A massive nuclear explosion went off. Wind, dirt, and smoke flew in all directions. The resultant mushroom cloud formed and just like that, the end was here.

Inside the Minot Air Force Base in North Dakota, the corpses of soldiers and other military personnel littered the base, presumably succumbed to hunger or radiation poisoning or both. Corpses lay all over the place where they fell. Firing mechanisms were still online and working automatically. In these nuclear silos, all the people were dead...

...but outside, the missiles were *still* firing. The ground in the vicinity had been charred and blasted to hell and back. But nuclear missiles were still lifting off into what used to be the Earth's atmosphere. It was the same for bases elsewhere on Earth, from the NAS Sigonella Base in Sicily to the Negev Nuclear Research Center in Israel to the Qinling mountain range base in China.

Hundreds of years later, the Earth had become bereft of its blue-greenness. All the missiles had fired and exploded and blasted the world into something even worse than pre-history. The space around the Earth was now littered with the planet's dirt that had risen into the exosphere. There were no clouds any longer to block the view of the dead world when seen from space.

"Even if all human life is snuffed out," Whisenhunt's voice guided the tour of the apocalypse. "Our poor old Earth will remain behind."

A destroyed continent had the appearance and consistency of a chocolate candy bar. There was no grass, only dirt and varying shades of brown. The nearby ocean looked like a massive mud puddle. The dirty water still, however, rolled against the shoreline. The land itself was nothing more than a never ending wasteland.

"Time won't stop just because we're gone," Whisenhunt explained. "There will be few changes on our battered planet for centuries to come. Life would eventually reform and return..."

The land on this continent was cracked and baked like bent shingles. It was a dingy, desolate hellscape in all directions.

"...But nothing will be beautiful ever again."

There was some *thing* moving in the background. As it approached, it could be seen to be some kind of female malformed being. It had the overall appearance and dimensions of a primate, but that of something in which a human being had been warped. The body was covered with lesions and tumor-like growths caused by intense radioactivity. It was just horribly scarred and mutated beyond recognition as being human. This female was as thin as a skeleton and moved disjointedly. It had no sexually identifiable traits other than long tufts of hair on the back of its misshapen head. This was a molted human.

The she-thing moved awkwardly on all fours, then eventually reared up shakily on its hind legs. It nearly fell over but managed to catch itself and wobbled forward. It looked skyward and seemed to groan but no voice came out of its mouth. Many of the teeth that should've been in the mouth were gone.

Nearby, another molted human wobbled along, except it looked a little different. It was smaller and had shorter hair than the first thing. This, in actuality, was its child.

A large snake wiggled in the dirt, dramatically, like it was dying. The first being caught sight of it. Its eyes widened and it silently gasped. As it dropped down on all fours again in an effort to move more quickly toward the snake, the child-thing was already charging ahead on all fours.

The child-thing managed to lay its distorted hands on the snake, but its parent tackled it, causing it to lose its grip and drop the snake. The two beings grappled with each other, mumbling incoherently. They fell to the ground and started going for each other's throats, rolling around like two fighting children, biting at each other's fragile bodies.

The snake, meanwhile, managed to wiggle away to go die in peace. That was, until a *third* molted human staggering in the distance caught sight of a potential fresh meal... and if it was lucky, a second and third as well.

[gotcha] CHAPTER 13 - The Choice is Yours

Back at the meeting in D.C, the Congress-people on hand listened astutely to Whisenhunt's pleas. Most looked terrified. Others were just concerned. Still others—like Senator Pfeiser—wore an expression of "yeah, right." President Cady looked especially worried.

"What was that about a whale monster?" one representative whispered to their neighbor.

"None of this has happened yet," Whisenhunt brought the audience back to a safer reality. "It may never happen. None of us knows the future. But with the problems currently facing us, such things *could* happen! Madame President Cady, you may be a human being like the rest of us, but you still have a responsibility. It's your job to make sure that these things don't come to pass. Otherwise, we're accelerating towards the end of our time on Earth!"

Cady took in every word that the doctor said.

"Madame President," he continued. "I implore you to enact policies of compassion and understanding. At least then, we can all live with hope. Please choose utopia over Armageddon... Thank you." Whisenhunt stepped down from the podium and went back to sit with his family.

There were audible murmurs from others in attendance but little else. Phoebe looked around the immediate area, nonplussed at the lack of response to her father. Whisenhunt just blankly stared ahead as if he had traumatized himself.

Madame President Cady rose to her feet, adjusted her business suit, then approached the podium.

"At the present as Dr. Whisenhunt has said," Cady leaned into the microphone as she began. "America is my responsibility. An America that the whole world is looking to as an example. The U.S., as it stands today, is in very dire straights. But I will try my best to put it back on the right path. This—like so many other things—will be no easy task. But America must step in to help lead the rest of the world out of its present crisis. But I will need assistance in bringing our country back to its admirable status. And today I am asking for that assistance. For far too long, the people have done nothing. People who have, in their power, the ability to change the world more than anyone in my cabinet. More than Republicans or Democrats together... In comparison, I and my cabinet are completely powerless. Without them, I have no support, no ability to rule, no ability to govern, and no ability to help. You are the people who represent the greater America. You are the ones who reserve all the power to change our country's troubled course. You are the only ones with the ability to change anything. A government has, at the most, very limited power. Without the support of the people though, a government such as ours is completely powerless to act. But with the support from yourselves and everyone else in the country, we may be able to overcome our present crisis and set our nation back on the right track again. For far too long now, we've pretended that we could solve our problems ourselves, without the trust of our citizens. Is it mankind's destiny to share the dinosaurs' fate? I should hope not, but they existed on the Earth much longer than man has and they're still gone. But I hope it's not too late to ask... Right now, I am asking for your support. Now is the time for America to rise up as an example for the rest of the world to get behind."

As Madame President Cady spoke, the listening audience began to think about their fellow countrymen. About the basic life of people in America...

...a crowd in a crowded city moving about their day peacefully.

"With all of your help," the president continued. "We can get going in the right direction again. It will take lots of hard work on all our parts to accomplish what we have to. And if we fail to accomplish what is needed of us, then the very future of mankind is in question."

...a mother washed her newborn child.

...fishermen pulled in their catch of the day.

...a little girl played with a group of pigeons that had congregated around a sidewalk.

...groups of green trees swayed in the breeze.

...a father carried his young son through a crowd of people at an amusement park.

...a thin mist veiled the top of a very large mountain.

...a young woman and her boyfriend ran together along the shores of a beach as the sun went down in the horizon.

...a baseball player smacked a homerun, leading the cheering crowd to roar. A young boy with a baseball glove in the stands managed to catch the homerun, causing the crowd to cheer even more.

...a cute young boy wore an oversized black cowboy hat and jostled about like he was riding a horse while his single mother worked at her computer at home.

...a couple of newlyweds posed for their wedding photo in total elation.

...clean water drifted in against a sandy beach.

...a small baby slept peacefully in a miniature chair.

...several boys raced down a sidewalk.

...a young couple kissed each other as they transversed shops in a strip mall.

...tree limbs swayed in the breeze as clear, bright sunlight shined through.

...a baby yawned, then turned inward toward the safety of his mother.

...a young mother shopping in a grocery store snatched up several tomatoes for cooking as she listened to music through earbuds.

...a crowd of people danced in the streets of New Orleans at Mardi Gras.

"This is a fact, and which way things go is wholly dependent on us," Cady explained. "We hold in our hands the ability to change the future for the better. So use that ability for the sake of our culture, for the sake of our traditions, but most importantly of all, do it for the sake of our children and for our children's children. Do your part to ensure that the future people of our country have a habitable place to grow up and live in. Without it, there may be no place for our future generations to even come into. Without it, everything may come to an end before our future generations have a chance at all. The human spirit is the most powerful tool we have. So use it... for our sake and for the sake of everyone on this planet. What's more, *you* must take action! Our entire future as a species hangs in the balance and you are the only ones who can act to ensure it..." The president looked around to everyone in the room. "Thank you," she whispered into the microphone.

The entire room broke into applause. The weight of the moment was too much for Whisenhunt. A tear fell down his face as he realized that finally after all these decades, *somebody* actually listened.

"Maybe there's some hope for us after all," Whisenhunt's mind spoke to him.

Later that evening on Capitol Hill, the entirety of Washington D.C. was shut down in an attempt to better the environment. People were nowhere to be found. Cars were not driving. Streets were empty.

The sun was going down in the far distance. A single, red balloon floated innocuously across the sky. On the ground below, Richard Whisenhunt and his children Jonathan and Phoebe—who was carrying his sleeping new granddaughter tightly in her grasp against her chest—walked down a main city street, each with their arms around the other, heading off to face the future.

THE END

This is a fictional story
but it is not just an imaginary world.
It should never be like this.
That is our wish for the future.

这是一个虚构的故事
但这不仅仅是一个想象的世界。
它不应该是这样的。
这是我们对未来的愿望。

Esta es una historia ficticia.
pero no es solo un mundo imaginario.
Nunca deberia ser asi.
Ese es nuestro deseo para el futuro.

Ceci est une histoire fictive
mais ce n'est pas seulement un monde imaginaire.
Cela ne devrait jamais etre comme ça.
C'est notre souhait pour l'avenir.

यह एक काल्पनकि कहानी है
लेकनि यह सरिफ एक काल्पनकि दुनयिा नहीं है.
ऐसा कभी नहीं होना चाहएि.
भवषियि के लएि यही हमारी कामना है.

هذه قصة خيالية
لكنه ليس مجرد عالم خيالي.
ال ينبغي أبدا أن يكون مثل اذا.
وذذه هي رغبتنا في المستقبل

これは虚構の物語りである。
だがたんなる想像の世界ではない。
こうあってはならない——
それが我々の願いである。

Это вымышленная история
но это не просто воображаемый мир.
Так быть никогда не должно.
Это наше желание на будущее.

Esta e uma historia ficticia
mas nao e apenas um mundo imaginario.
Nunca deveria ser assim.
Esse e o nosso desejo para o futuro.

이것은 허구의 이야기입니다
하지만 그것은 단지 상상의 세계가 아닙니다.
결코 이렇게 되어서는 안 됩니다.
그것이 미래에 대한 우리의 소망입니다.

Dies ist eine fiktive Geschichte
aber es ist nicht nur eine imaginare Welt.
So sollte es nie sein.
Das ist unser Wunsch fur die Zukunft.

Other books in the Constantine Furman library:
A Greyer Shade of White (2017)
Damned Kids (2018)
Street Walkin' Man (2018)
A Specter Tale (2018) and sequels
   - *Another Specter Tale* (2019)
   - *A Specter Tale Continues* (2020)
   - *A Specter Tale Concludes: Requiem Mass for Natali*
    (2021)
Constantine Furman's The Life of Marta (2019)
Giant Monster Farmarna (2020) and sequels
   - *Farmarna's Monster Martial Law* (2021)
   - *Dragora, the Monster Goddess* (2022)
   - *Farmarna's Counterattack* (2023)
   - *Monster of Monsters, Tiamat* (2024)
The Unofficial Tokusatsu Fan's Handbook for Gamera,
   Super Monster (2021)
Facts and Figures of Japanese Monsters: 1954-2012 (2022)

Coming Later:
Monster Defense Forces
Princess of Darkness
The Marvelous Witch of the West
Natali Has Risen from the Grave

Made in the USA
Coppell, TX
16 December 2025

66131619R00094